PRAISE FOR *As the An*

"In *As the Andes Disappeared*, Caroline Dawson achieves a rare feat—the expression of exile as experienced by a child. Poignantly, vividly, through Anita Anand's perfect translation of Dawson's elegant and easy-flowing prose, we are drawn into the world of a girl plucked out of Chile and its overwhelming *cordillera*, and dropped into the emotional, physical, and linguistic space of 1980s Québec. Memory, whether inherited, remembered, lived, or made anew, is at the core of this utterly human and beautifully written novel. An essential addition to Canadian culture."
—BEATRIZ HAUSNER, author of *She Who Lies Above*

"This beautiful, poetic book vividly captures an immigrant experience and drew me in from the very first sentence to the very last. As an immigrant myself, I saw my own experiences mirrored similarly. I'm so grateful to have read this and I hope you will, too."
—HASAN NAMIR, author of *Umbilical Cord* and *War/Torn*

"The power of this largely autobiographical novel lies in its refusal to let anger yield to gratitude. Nor is gratitude permitted to soften the rage of knowing that the comfort of the rich continues to be built with the egregiously paid labour of those who cannot push back."
—*Le Devoir*

"There are books that make us better people, and Dawson's is among them."
—MICHEL MARC BOUCHARD, le Combat national des livres de Radio-Canada

"When exactly does a child from Chile, an immigrant to Québec, cease including the Andes in the background of her drawings? What parts of us are erased as we construct our identities? With sensitivity, humour, and engaging lucidity, Dawson's autobiographical novel shows us that there are many lived realities and that it is essential to be attentive to everyone's experience. To read *As the Andes Disappeared* is to acquire tools to understand the Other and to confront one's own perceptions of society."
—MARC-ÉTIENNE BRIEN, Librairie Biblairie GGC

As the Andes Disappeared

Caroline Dawson

translated by Anita Anand

Book*hug Press
Toronto 2023
Literature in Translation Series

FIRST ENGLISH EDITION
Published originally under the title *Là où je me terre* Caroline Dawson et les
Éditions du remue-ménage, 2020
English translation © 2023 by Anita Anand

Library and Archives Canada Cataloguing in Publication
Title: As the Andes disappeared : a novel / Caroline Dawson ;
    translated by Anita Anand.
Other titles: Là où je me terre. English
Names: Dawson, Caroline, 1979- author. | Anand, Anita (Translator),
    translator.
Description: Translation of: Là où je me terre.
Identifiers: Canadiana (print) 20230220940 | Canadiana (ebook) 20230220959
   ISBN 9781771668613 (softcover)
   ISBN 9781771668620 (EPUB)
   ISBN 9781771668637 (PDF)
Classification: LCC PS8607.A9614 L313 2023 | DDC C843/.6—dc23

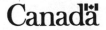

The production of this book was made possible through the generous assist-
ance of the Canada Council for the Arts and the Ontario Arts Council.
Book*hug Press also acknowledges the support of the Government of Canada
through the Canada Book Fund and the Government of Ontario through the
Ontario Book Publishing Tax Credit and the Ontario Book Fund.

Book*hug Press acknowledges that the land on which we operate is the trad-
itional territory of many nations, including the Mississaugas of the Credit, the
Anishnabeg, the Chippewa, the Haudenosaunee, and the Wendat peoples.
We recognize the enduring presence of many diverse First Nations, Inuit, and
Métis peoples and are grateful for the opportunity to meet, work, and learn
on this territory.

CONTENTS

For my queen, Bérénice

PROLOGUE

Residencia en la tierra[1]

THE FIRST TIME I DECIDED NOT TO KILL MYSELF, I WAS SEVEN years old.

It was summer in the Southern Hemisphere, December 1986. In Valparaíso, the land of sandy dust that infiltrates poorly insulated old stone houses and sticks to all the furniture. Our house stood—I'm not sure how—on one of the hundreds of slopes of one of the dozens of hills in one of Chile's big cities. It seemed unstable and rickety, yet it resisted each earthquake that regularly shook it and all the other crappy houses in our poor neighbourhood. It moved in sync with the Earth itself, and I with it.

I whirled around on the top floor, the only one that let in a little light. Our house was old, dim, and shabby, like all the others on the steep hill we called our street. The ocean wind knocked at the windows, snuck inside even when everything was shut. My parents called me from their bedroom, had me join them on the gigantic ocean liner they used as a bed. It was probably just a queen, but to my young eyes, it was an enormous island. The soft light of dawn on the white sheets, the warmth of their still, sleepy bodies, the lovely languor of early morning: it was bliss, lying there between them. I rolled from one side to the other, seeking attention. Until they grew subdued and said those sharp, stark words that divided time into a before and an after, a past and a future. They announced their decision, and I froze; time stood still, the future was suspended. A pivotal moment, words like blades, like an axe splitting a log.

I don't know what those words were. They've been obliterated, as have almost all my memories of the country where I was born. And yet, I did spend a good part of my childhood in Chile. It's where I first went to school, learned to read and write with words like *mi mamá*,* loved my family and my friends. Like all Chileans, I played with my *balero*,† my *trompo*,‡ with kites made from old newspaper. My life was carefree and happy despite the disappearances, detentions, tortures, and concentration camps of which I'd heard nothing more than murmurs, half-spoken whispers. I spent seven years under a dictatorship in a divided, unstable country, and I barely remember anything apart from this turning point in our lives. That moment and then everything that followed it.

They told me that in a few days we would leave the country to seek refuge in Canada—forever. Fear seized me then, in the same place it sometimes still does: in my stomach. Stunned by the immutability of this decision, I didn't say a word, didn't ask a single question. I was clearly aware of the seriousness of this moment and of my complete powerlessness to change anything. I looked at my pudgy hands and wondered if Canadian children also had dirt under their fingernails or if everything over there was immaculate.

My parents left the room, left me alone to come to terms with their decision, and with the magnitude of my own emotions. On this bed-island in this stone house that I'd believed to be as eternal

---

* My mother.

† A game with a cup on top of a stick attached to a ball on a string.

‡ Chilean spinning top.

as a rock, the floor seemed to quake until it disappeared under my feet, and I wallowed in my despair. They'd been categorical: "We're leaving the country and never coming back."

"Never ever?"

"Never ever."

"Not even for birthdays? Not even for school vacations? Or Christmas?"

"No. Not even for births. Not even for burials."

"And what about all the people we love?"

"We'll keep loving them. From far away."

The foundations of what I'd thought was my life were giving way. Could we really love from far away? My world had crumbled. In a single fleeting moment, something swung out of balance, and the universe, as I had known it, turned to vapour and slipped through my grubby fingers.

I took stock of everything I'd be leaving behind, feeling as if I were the one being dispossessed. My pencils, my drawings. My notebooks, my classmates. My book of stickers, my school. My skipping rope, my friends. My tree, my cousin. My pebble collection, *mi abuelita.** My hopscotch, my mother tongue. My hula hoops, my certainties. My grandfather and my dog, who both died before I could see them again. Final farewells dragged out of me, forced, torn from the bottom of my throat. *A Dios.*

I was suffocating. I opened the window. The sun blinded me. Below, the orange ground, the grime, the mangy stray dogs. Farther off, the avocado trees, the Pacific Ocean, the Andes. I'd never see this horizon again; I'd never have this view as a reference point. The heavy finality and the pain of inevitability crushed my lungs. The air deserted me.

I hoisted myself onto the window ledge. I looked at the ground from the top of my cliff. It didn't shrink back; it invited me. *Jump, little one. The life you used to have no longer exists. Say goodbye. No, don't say goodbye, just jump and it'll be over. Leave without saying*

---

* My grandmother.

anything to anyone. Jump before your parents come back. They told you, Chile, it's over. The world as you know it doesn't exist anymore. Seize the moment and jump. So that life as you've loved it remains within you when you return to the earth.

I would die there, between the cordillera and the sea, dust in my mouth, anguish in my guts.

I didn't jump.

Not out of apathy or laziness. Faced with the call of the void, I made my first important decision, the most important one. The life that stretched out in front of me took up all the space. I'd just turned seven years old and made my first leap of faith in favour of the world that would henceforth reveal itself as a foreign perspective, an unfamiliar point of view. I didn't know that I would unconsciously renew this choice every day, even in dark moments, in times of upheaval, in bleak fog.

I didn't kill myself in that room, but something that had existed died. I tore myself from my past at the same time as I was being uprooted. From then on, I kept only two or three muddled memories. Almost nothing remained from Chile, neither in our suitcases nor in my head. From my buried past, I would retain almost nothing: foggy fragments I happened to remember, stories in ruins, memories in ashes. The only thing that endured was a posture, a relationship to the real world and a way of being in the world: embrace existence, even if that necessitated completely transfiguring it. My death wish crashed to the ground as I went into survival mode.

PART I

Sometimes in America, race is class.
—Chimamanda Ngozi Adichie

In a big, sea-blue Boeing[2]

THE DAYS PRECEDING OUR DEPARTURE WERE ENTIRELY taken up with preparations. My mother wrote lists on anything she could find; crumpled slips of paper littered our house, the same house that was so quickly clearing us out. Our vacated furniture gave way to sudden emptiness, and yet there was no space for my childish fears as I tried to both understand our present and glimpse our future. Although I'd never been on a plane, I have no memory of being excited to board the flying monster that would take us to Canada. I couldn't fathom how those huge engines would manage to stay suspended in the air with so many people and suitcases strapped to their bellies. Faced with my parents' resolute march toward our new life, I was floored by the very idea of this flight; it presented itself as a metaphor for all that eluded me.

I saw how my parents' worries overshadowed the last days of December. I didn't talk about it; I kept it to myself. It was only once inside the plane, after the flight attendants completed their safety demonstration, that I—immobile, the seat belt tight around my waist—finally fell sick. My body spewed out all its worries in an endless stream of diarrhea. My poor parents had to spend most of this trip that was bringing them to a new, unknowable life taking turns going back and forth between the airplane's tiny bathrooms and their uncomfortable seats, so that their daughter could empty herself of her anxiety.

After the third time, my mother said, "You know, you can ask me if you have any questions."

"Okay. Is Canada far away?"

"Yes."

"How far?"

"About nine thousand kilometres."

"What are kilometres?"

"It's what we use to measure long distances."

"Oh. So nine thousand kilometres is far?"

"Yes."

"But are we going to get there before tomorrow?"

"No. When we get there, it'll already be tomorrow."

"What?"

"When we get there, it'll already be tomorrow."

"But then we'll miss Christmas!"

"No, no. We'll celebrate Christmas on the plane. You can sleep now, and tomorrow we'll be there."

My parents had actually chosen December 24 to begin our family's exile. Could that be right? We wouldn't have Christmas that year? Imprisoned mid-flight in that huge plane, I went on with my list of questions. Does the sky have a middle? How does the plane stay up in the air? Could it fall? Where exactly are we when we're in the air? And especially, how was Santa Claus going to find us?

That's when I realized I was nowhere. Out the window, way down below me, the only things visible were clouds. Nothing in front of us, nothing behind us, the world had disappeared from my sight, carrying with it, it seemed, people living there, playing soccer, hugging, kissing, mourning their dead or departed loved ones.

From up there I saw only clouds, thick clouds that took up all the space and obscured my vision.

"What are clouds, Mama?"

"Water vapour. Go to sleep now, my baby."

"But how does water vapour stay up in the sky?"

"I don't know. Ask Papa."

My father, with his wrinkled forehead and haggard features, was too far away, both physically and in his own thoughts, for me to ask him anything. To me, clouds would always remain air, emptiness, nothing. A kind of nothingness that began to weigh heavily on my shoulders, knotting itself into a clump, an icy mass, like the one in my little stomach. How the heck was Santa Claus going to find us through these clouds? My questions accumulated in my throat. I was having trouble breathing through all this fog. Once again, it had to come out; I threw up. Over and over again, until there was nothing left.

In addition to the stale air and breath of five hundred passengers crammed together, the plane now also smelled of vomit.

"Can we open a window, Mama?"

"No, we can't."

"Why not?"

"They're sealed shut."

"Sealed shut? Why?"

"Because of the air pressure. If we opened a window, the people would get sucked outside."

"Outside? So they'd die?"

"Yes, they'd die."

"So we can't open anything?"

"Not while we're flying, no. Now say your bedtime prayer and try to sleep."

The altitude overwhelmed me. The pressure snuck into my empty stomach and made it heave. A gap in a door, a crack in the windows, could send us falling to our deaths. We'd accepted that risk; my parents had bet on the unknown—the void ahead of us— to save us from our *before*.

At the age of seven, I became profoundly aware that it was possible to leave everything and never return.

At the age of seven, I learned to say "adieu" and not "bye-bye," not "see you tomorrow," not "see you soon," not "goodbye," not even "see you again one of these days." Adieu, which means farewell forever, "to God," 'til never again.

At the age of seven, I stopped believing in God and in a predetermined fate.

At the age of seven, on a plane for the first time, I pretended to pray; I'd figured out that we were the ones who decided. We could just ditch everything and start a whole new life. But I continued to wonder how, if nobody could open anything, Santa Claus would manage to come in.

Finally, I succumbed to exhaustion and my questions faded away. I was asleep at last, but my mother's worries were far from over. She'd had to plan every detail of this giant leap into the unknown. Among the thousands of things she'd had to think about—the passports, visas, clothes for winters she was completely unfamiliar with, our safety, saying goodbye to her own mother, to her sister, to her brothers, to her friends, to her life, the police, the dictatorship—there had also been the unrelenting needs of children, which never disappear, not even when you're fleeing a country that is ripping apart—snacks, presents from Santa Claus. It moves me to imagine how, as she was cramming our lives into a few suitcases bought on credit, she took the trouble to hide some toys in the hand luggage. In the middle of this voyage into political exile, hanging on to a bit of normalcy for her terrified children meant that, among a great many slips of paper, she included a reminder to bring along the list for Santa.

When I woke up to the stale air of the plane, a brand-new Barbie was lying next to me. She was fresh, pink, clean, radiant, and perfect. She smiled at me. As my appetite slowly returned amid the rattling of the breakfast trays, I began to believe we'd land somewhere after all. Despite the knot in my throat, I took a bite of the bread that had been placed before me. It went down; I didn't throw up. I put some butter on it. It was good. I'd just turned seven, my mouth was full, and I had a new Barbie, a real one finally, not some cheap imitation.

I straddled two worlds now: I didn't believe in God anymore, but I'd keep believing in Santa Claus for a long time. Too long— *years*—until I was finally told that he didn't exist. Just before it would have gotten really embarrassing.

Northern stars remind us of death[3]

THE LANDING WAS ABRUPT. AN ICE STORM HAD HIT QUÉBEC, and, as if to warn us not to count on our expectations for our new lives, we were told that our flight to Montreal would be diverted to Toronto. My father requested political asylum at Canadian customs on behalf of all the other refugees on our flight. He was the only one among them who could speak English. A series of measures—established according to impersonal rules that had already been applied a thousand times before, to those who had preceded us—now came down on us. From that point on, from the moment we had to leave the long, main queue, from those first looks exchanged between us, the asylum seekers—determination in our stomachs, fear in our voices—and the skeptical customs official, I knew we wouldn't be allowed a single misstep.

There was a guy behind us, wide-eyed at the scene unfolding before him. He was obviously just back from a business trip, and still a bit tipsy from the little glass of wine on the plane. Shaken by the small human drama he was witnessing, he looked around for an ally, a normal traveller in the crowd. No luck—nothing but Chileans and a scruffy young backpacker returning from his first trip to South America. The two of them exchanged looks of astonishment, as well as a few sentences punctuated by the words "*Oh mon dieu.*"

The *oh mon dieu*s multiplied when they saw the customs official call for backup, suspecting the five members of my family, as well as all the other silent people who had left the line, of somehow putting their lives in danger. Their stories couldn't have been more different from ours: a loved one undoubtedly waited for them just outside, someone who'd listen as they recounted all of this, waving their hands, full of emotion as they made their way home, to their own houses, while we remained still, frozen in time and space, feeling like trespassers and thieves in this country that was not yet ours.

The airport police sent us into another room, the one at the back, invisible to ordinary travellers. We went through the little door, heads bowed, staring at the floor. The unfriendly man in the uniform failed to be moved by our story. *Our lives are in danger. We have three children. We are seeking refuge.* Words practised a million times. You'd think the world would stop turning for less than that, but no, he didn't even look at us. Sign here. Go wait over there until someone calls you. You will be interviewed. It will probably take a while. His glance at the clock, sigh, next.

Right behind our *thank you, thank you, thank you very much*: clenched teeth, bitten lips, balled fists, something like a choked scream in our throats. But refugees can't talk.

Or at least we didn't say anything unless we were asked to. We were obedient, docile. We waited patiently, answered their questions. We said thank you, swallowing our spit, clutching our papers, and then we went to sit in the dingiest corner of the room. The room where we awaited our temporary verdict was drab, grey, soulless, overheated, and overfull with miserable, circumspect people like us. Dozens of terrorized yet expressionless human beings who had put their lives in the hands of these airport cops no one trusted, even if we'd been told that Canadian police were all right. We had our doubts: in Chile, the so-called peace officers were the ones who arrested, bludgeoned, tortured, and assassinated. The worker ants of the dictatorship. What were they protecting here?

Here, it really bugged them that it was December 25. We were making them work late on Christmas Day; it was annoying. *They could have picked some other day,* said the face of the officer who sighed noisily every five minutes, grumbling as if we'd ruined his Christmas on purpose, muttering things I couldn't understand, pointing at us. He refused to meet our eyes the entire time we stood in front of him. This kind of man, who looks away from people, who flees when confronted with human suffering, is the first type of person I ever hated. I swore I'd never forget his face, so I could hate him—and others of his ilk—my whole life.

Barely five years earlier, Québec had received a few dozen annual applications for refugee status. In December of 1986, more than 2,300 were filed. A week would not go by without the media bringing up this "crisis." Human beings were referred to as a problem to solve, and the Canadian government, under Brian Mulroney, implemented new policies seeking to limit the acceptance of asylum seekers. These policies were requested and welcomed by the province of Québec, under Robert Bourassa. Consequently, from the beginning of the 1990s, border controls grew tighter.

Among the 2,300 individuals fleeing persecution in their country of origin was my mother, Natalia. My father, Alfredo. My older brother Jim, who was fourteen years old. My younger brother Nicholas, who was four. And me, Caroline Dawson. Our first and last names were bellowed, summoning us to get in line for questioning.

Since the Geneva Convention was on our side, we were accepted on a provisional basis after the initial background checks. This allowed the time to undertake a long judicial process; it would be years before we could become permanent residents. The room was frighteningly dreary. We were chilled by the idea of change and petrified by uncertainty. Yet we held on, driven to survive on more stable ground, where shocks and tremors would be a thing of the past. For the first time, we were offered a choice, as if we were suddenly being acknowledged as individuals with the right to self-determination. Would you prefer to live in Toronto or take the next flight to Montreal?

Would other horizons have opened up had we stayed in Ontario? We'll never know. We made a decision based on not a hell of a lot—rumours of more generous social programs in Québec—and then we waited together in weary silence for the storm to pass. Toronto would remain a stopover for us. My parents might have chosen Montreal on a dime, but we did end up staying awhile.

Passe-Partout[4]

THE RAMADA HOTEL ON SHERBROOKE STREET, EAST OF Langelier Boulevard. I'll always remember the burgundy carpet that lined the entrance. The long staircase and its excessively steep steps. The reception counter with the scary people in uniforms behind it. The elevator, to the right of the dining room. The door of room 308. That room, our base camp, our temporary residence, our Canadian shanty. We'd looked everywhere before we figured out that it was on the third floor. As we came out of the elevator, we realized that an entire floor was set aside for refugees awaiting their status. It was full and overcrowded, mostly with Turks and their large families.

The Turks were crammed into rooms with six or seven people, two queen beds and a single bathroom. They had nothing to do and spent a lot of their time pacing up and down the hallways. Sometimes they'd just sit there, on the carpet. We didn't talk to each other much, as we didn't have a common language. Some of them would eat sunflower seeds, leaving bits everywhere. The first time we went to our room, we heard our feet go *crunch crunch*. It's horrible to say, but we looked down on our neighbours. There were so many of them, and they seemed so noisy and messy with those sunflower seeds. They provided the background noise to our situation, a soundtrack for our exile. We couldn't pretend to be on vacation at a hotel with those sunflower seed shells strewn all over the ground reminding us of where we really were.

When we got to room 308, my feet refused to move. All of us stopped, as if the act of unlocking the door and entering the room would cause the world to tip over, an abrupt shift that would some-how seal our fate. How to know if we'd made the right decisions? Nobody said anything. I think it was my father, firm and dispassion-ate, who broke the silence and opened the door to room 308. Who else but my dad, the man of the hour? Following behind the rest of my family, the only thing I saw was my mother's back. She was thirty-five years old at the time, with three kids and a shaky future that hinged on this little room key in a hotel filled with foreigners.

We gingerly entered the room, fear churning in our bellies. I'm saying *we*, but I had no idea what the other members of my family were experiencing. While we may have been walking together, faced with the unknown, I know each of us was alone. I wasn't watching the others: I was busy examining our room—and I felt relieved. Heated, not too small, pretty clean, no sunflower seeds on the floor. We ended up living there a month, but at the time I had no idea, didn't even know if we'd be able to stay there thirty minutes. The first things I noticed corresponded to two essential needs for the little girl I was then: the beds and the biggest television set I'd ever seen. Naturally, I raced over and turned it on.

On Radio-Québec, it was time for *Passe-Partout*. Three adults dressed like friendly circus performers were chatting together. I couldn't understand a thing, and that put me off. Puppets with squeaky voices appeared, as if to confirm that this show was not for me but for younger children. I waited, watched for a few more min-utes. I was about to change the channel when the smallest of the adults I'd seen earlier returned to the screen. She suddenly turned toward me.

I didn't know what her words meant, but her expressive eyes dove right into mine. Her words were indistinct to me, none reached me, but still, the first person who looked me in the eyes and spoke to me in Québec was the actress Marie Eykel in the role of Passe-Partout. I couldn't make out the meaning of her words, but I identified with her unhappiness. She was anxious, tormented. She looked me right in the face and I saw my own troubled feelings reflected back at me. I imagined that she was telling me about her sorrow, her fear, and I understood her. She was kind and gentle as she spoke to me—and this managed to alleviate my apprehensions about the new life ahead of me. The carpet under my feet suddenly seemed more stable—somehow even rosier—and the background noise now seemed tinged with notes of empathy. Her voice soothed me, and I realized I wasn't going to disintegrate. I could probably grow roots here too, even if I was a bit wilted.

Cité libre[5]

WE'D SCARCELY LEFT A DICTATORSHIP BEHIND WHEN WE found ourselves locked up in a hotel, forbidden from leaving its premises. An iron fence, tall and grey like in prisons, served as our legal boundary. Such a confinement was the norm. Refugees were made to stay at a hotel while background checks were done, and this could range from a few days to a few weeks. They ordered us to never leave the area, fearing what would happen if we became undocumented migrants escaping national control. We therefore stayed confined for weeks at the Ramada, this hotel that was both asylum and prison. The slightest breach could cost us a direct expulsion back to our country of origin, without a trial of any sort.

But when there are three kids in the same room for days with no idea of when they'll be let out, they'll scream, they'll yell, and they'll be in perpetual motion; it's narrow and cramped, they want to go outside, especially since it was precisely freedom they'd been promised as they were leaving. Our parents let us twist around on our chairs, jump on the beds, sing at the top of our lungs in the

bath, but we knew the permissions we were granted were fake free-
doms, little allowances to keep us from going berserk with boredom.
Everything was regulated: we ate when the hotel cafeteria allowed
it, watched what the television showed us, walked up and down the
gloomy third-floor hallway crushing sunflower seeds under our feet.
My parents did what they could to distract us. We'd gotten into the
habit of walking around the grounds of the hotel, but this was our
first Canadian winter, and the cold was one more obstacle when we
wanted to venture outside. Anyway, the sight of the fence rendered
the air unbreathable: it reminded us that there was a threshold
beyond which our movements were prohibited.

On a relatively mild day, when the snow had melted a little,
we decided to go out and walk around the hotel parking lot. My
mother suddenly opened her mouth as if to scream. Along with the
other members of our family, I followed her amazed gaze and saw
what she did, the hole at the end of the fence. A fairly large, visible
gap created by some other people who'd preceded us. It seemed
to dare us to approach. It was calling to us; there was no way to
unsee it. It was there, conspicuous, defiant, and undisciplined, as if
to mock the mere existence of the restrictions.

Who had dared? Where were they from? And where were they
today? Were they still at the hotel? Sent back to their country? Or
integrated into society as if nothing had happened, as if they hadn't
cheated the system? Did they remember this affront? There was
a hole; it was undeniable, and it was just big enough for human
beings to crawl through on their knees. Those people had invited us.
The hole was so clearly inviting us that it became intolerable. We
all glanced around: no hotel staff in view, no surveillance cameras
that could identify us. The only thing we didn't know was whether
it represented light or mortal danger.

What would we do? It's not as if we could decide to go to
the casino or to La Ronde. We were on the inhospitable Langelier
Boulevard, without a car, a bus pass, or money. What would be
the point of escaping? Were we really going to defy the rules to
parade our quiet misery around for the world to see? Here, on this

soulless boulevard brimming with Chinese buffets? We'd observe a few unremarkable, indifferent strangers with interchangeable faces briskly walking by, like in any big city. Was it really worth risking everything for that privilege?

But at the same time, wasn't that precisely why we'd fled Chile? To risk everything, to breathe in all the seasons, to see the horizon spread out in front of us, for a draft of freedom? I think the abject futility of the gesture also gave it its beauty. The gaping hole calling to us transformed the fence from an obstacle to a watershed, a beginning.

We all crouched down and, one after another, went through to the other side. Even if we'd already been outdoors, for the first time we really got out, escaped, as if we'd crossed the threshold that separated us from our future.

We wandered around the grey, concrete-heavy area for a few minutes. There was something reassuring in the incessant noise of all these automobiles: they didn't care about us. Strangely, even if the air was colder and the wind more violent on these city streets, I could breathe more easily here.

I wasn't the only one—we all repeated our escape. In fact, we went out every day. Each of us, to remind ourselves that we were still alive. Every morning the hole in the fence provided us with a window onto the world.

No one ever saw us, even though our recurrent recklessness ended up widening the hole. Maybe for those who would come after us.

Liberty isn't a brand of yogourt[6]

WHEN WE LEFT THE HOTEL WHERE WE'D BEEN CONFINED, we had nowhere to go. While we waited to find a small apartment in the northern part of the city, we squatted for a few days with the only acquaintances my parents had, a family of Chileans. The father had been in love with my favourite aunt in his youth. Despite their breakup, he'd continued to have a friendly relationship with our family. He came by from time to time to say hi to my grandmother, as is the custom with most Latinos. In exchange, she gave him advice and blessings. His visits had ceased when he emigrated to Canada, where he met another woman, also a Chilean exile. The couple had since had two children, two little girls the same age as my little brother and me, both born in Montreal.

The younger one was the more adorable of the two. Small, sweet, a bit pale, with short, fine hair adorned with a bobby pin to the right side of her wispy bangs. I can see her again as a four-year-old, always dressed in little pink or yellow dresses that were too short on her, her cheeks rosy with mischief. She was on the plump side, the perfect image of kids in French books from between the wars, and I don't think it would be wrong to say that she was, even at the age of four, a bit of a *bonne vivante*. Like a good Chilean for whom there are only two options: a fat body or a thin one. Her mother tried in vain to get her to lose a few pounds or to at least not gain any more, with modest diets and light privations, but the little girl always managed to sneak a piece of bread when the grown-ups had their backs turned. A food-lover myself, I joined her in her frivolous filching, even though I much preferred playing with her big sister, the thin one.

Today I can imagine the chaos this family endured as they sheltered another under their roof. Five people, near strangers, with whom they shared neither blood nor a last name, suddenly invading their privacy, sharing an apartment that was already two small for them. Suddenly, they found themselves at a numeric disadvantage in their own household. Everyone had to shower in the same bathroom, brush their teeth at the same sink, eat their breakfast at the same table, make polite chit-chat while standing in line, before the first cup of coffee, for the first pee of the day in the only bathroom. My parents will always feel indebted to them, and I'm sure they'll still be thanking them in their graves. And they're right.

For my brothers and me, even if it wasn't easy, it was still a lot better. Of course, we weren't at home, but we found ourselves in a place filled with life, not confined to an anonymous hotel room with no room to run, shout, or play. When we walked in the apartment, we didn't hear *crunch crunch* anymore; we might have heard the noise of our own *pan con palta** crumbs. We were able to go outside now, leave footprints in the snow, even if they vanished with the next snowfall. We could, if we wished, exist in the outside world, even if we usually preferred to stay inside together.

We also finally had access to a refrigerator. At the hotel, when my parents had ventured through the fence to buy a few pieces of fruit and a hunk of cheese on special, they'd put them on the

---

* Bread with avocado.

windowsill outside. Everything had frozen, and I saw my mother's eyes fill with helpless tears.

Like all active children, I was constantly famished, but I was too shy to help myself to a snack between meals. It would have called for a degree of self-assurance I never managed to have in that environment. I could, therefore, claim it was hunger, a primitive and visceral need, that sent me to the fridge the first time without an invitation—but it would be untrue. If after a few days I dared to open the fridge door, it was just that I succumbed to an irrepressible curiosity.

There, among the vegetables, eggs, and bags of milk was a container of vanilla yogourt. It had been weeks since I'd eaten yogourt. We used to eat it every day back in Chile and there hadn't been any at the hotel. On the top, the word LIBERTÉ, like a celebration of what I was up to. I immediately understood, as *libertad** was one of the words my mother had taught me to write. It was like I was being invited, in capital letters, to open the container. I took it out, repeating the word *liberté* to myself; I already had a sense of drama. As I sniffed it, I told myself that it was almost as if it wasn't me who had discovered it; it was like *it* found *me*. Maybe I was just lacking stimulation, but I was really quite discombobulated.

I ate the vanilla yogourt with my eyes closed, and with a delicious sense of doing something forbidden. It tasted fresh, creamy, sweet, exquisite. Each spoonful was a pleasure and delight that I experienced with an almost religious fervour. And what was truly exceptional is that I experienced this alone, in an apartment that currently sheltered nine people. I would have taken another helping, but when I turned around, I saw the little girl and her flabbergasted face.

She didn't say anything, at least not with her mouth, but her eyes were filled with judgment. She stared me down, pinching her little lips, her hands on her hips like a strict schoolmarm: her whole body was shouting. I was still holding the yogourt container in my

---

* Freedom.

left hand and I knew that one false move would make her yell for real. She didn't turn around and go away until she'd seen me carefully place the container back in its rightful place, on the top shelf of the fridge. Then, nothing. Radio silence on my behaviour.

That evening, I heard the little girl and her mother talking about yogourt-gate. They didn't know I was in the bathroom, which was next to the kitchen. The little one told her everything: my crime, its discovery, our silent duel, her victory. Her mother listened to her; her tone was calm, patient, and reassuring. And then the words that felt like a great violent shove: "*Mami, quiero que se vayan. Se van a comer toda nuestra comida.*" * Rage audible between the little food enthusiast's teeth.

"*Lo sé, mi hija, lo sé.*" †

Mortified, I stayed in the bathroom, immobile and ashamed. We'd just arrived, and the smallest member of the family, the sweet, charming one, had already had enough of me. I'd always be an intruder. The only way I could take up space would be as a fugitive, sneaking around.

I never again asked them for yogourt, and if anyone offered me any I'd decline, claim I wasn't hungry. Instead, I got into the habit of filching small portions and eating it in secret, usually directly from the container. In fact, I never again asked for anything at all, and forbidding myself to beg for the slightest thing became a way of life.

It's still something I do today—first turn down what I'm offered, reject the things I'm given, in order to later enjoy them discreetly or even hog them on the sly. After that day of stolen liberty, I learned to see things by peeking through doors and to walk around on tiptoes so no one would notice me. Surreptitiously look over my shoulder to make sure no one saw me. Fragile and furtive as a fleeting moment.

---

* "Mommy, I want them to go now. They're going to eat all our food."
† "I know, my daughter, I know."

This is the story of the little beaver[7]

I DON'T KNOW HOW, BUT MY PARENTS LAID THEIR HANDS ON a four-and-a-half[8] in Ahuntsic, in an apartment building full of Latinos. Everyone was Spanish-speaking except the janitor—a spindly old Québécoise with a voice hoarse from the lung cancer that would kill her a few years later. In the building's squalid lobby there were always a few gossips hanging around. Also, dozens of old flyers. And the leftover smells of fried foods and poverty. Our smell.

Our apartment was furnished with the various disparate donations gathered by a social worker known to all of Montreal's Spanish-speaking refugees. As soon as we moved in, my parents were eligible for free French classes. Québec had just made it easier for immigrants to access orientation and training centres—famously known as COFI[9]—with a big ad campaign in the newspapers, where they'd never stopped boasting their merits with respect to the integration of new arrivals. In theory, my parents could choose between studying French or working. But with three kids, it wasn't so straightforward. There was no way my parents would sit in a classroom while our old, noisy fridge—donated by some charitable soul—stayed empty. They had three mouths to feed, and since they couldn't speak French, they did what most refugees do: they found shit jobs where they didn't have to speak.

Between the factory, the housecleaning, and the restaurants, my parents worked days, evenings, nights, and weekends, alternating shifts, rarely less than twelve hours a day. I never heard them say they were tired, and it was only years later, looking through photographs of that time that I could see see how their young eyes were marked by dark circles of resignation. On the weekends, they caught up on some of the sleep they'd sold to their bosses. Seeing their bedroom door closed, my little brother and I didn't disturb them; instead, we turned to the television for company.

The TV showed us mostly Japanese cartoons, mostly dubbed into French. My favourites were without a doubt *Maya the Bee*,[10] *The Smoggies*,[11] *Sur la rue Tabaga*,[12] and *The Raccoons*, but we weren't that picky. We watched everything, even *Ovide and the Gang*,[13] *Seabert*,[14] *Mrs. Pepper Pot*,[15] and even *Hachi*[16] if we had to. We watched each show from beginning to end. Everything except *The Mysterious Cities of Gold*,[17] about travellers to sixteenth-century South America. I'm ashamed to say we turned the television off when that came on.

When we watched these weekend programs, the last things my little brother and I dreamed about were conquering Latin America, deciphering its secrets, or discovering its lost treasures. The truth is that my half-buried memories of the Andes cordillera made me sad. That wasn't a horizon I could allow myself to think about now. People like us, descended from the Incas and the European colonizers, now lived under dictatorship or in exile. Watching *The Mysterious Cities of Gold* could not help us understand our present environment or the one we'd left behind.

For us, in that little apartment where we got drunk on television, *Le petit castor* was much more relevant. The constant arguments, the frequent running away from home, the bad decisions, the emotional instability, the excessive reactions to unexpected events, the bad guys who come out of nowhere and get taught a good lesson.

We'd only been in Québec a few weeks; the show was predictable and we were able to get the gist of the stories. We didn't speak any French yet, apart from about ten words we'd learned from *Passe-Partout*. We didn't understand the show's opening credits, and although now it seems very clear to us that they were saying, "*C'est l'histoire du petit castor*," which meant, "This is the story of the little beaver"—what we heard was "*Alessona, petit castor*."

That morning, we'd sung, "*Alessona, petit castor*," together in a loop, at the top of our lungs, in the only space where we felt at home, the family four-and-a-half, while my parents tried to catch up on some sleep before one of them had to go do a night shift. As usual, nobody got up to tell us to be quiet.

Between two "*Alessona, petit castors*," we heard noises outside, kids laughing. We looked out the window and saw the neighbours playing in fluorescent snowsuits. They built a fort—in no time flat—and then went inside it. My little brother and I looked at each other. Their skills blew us away. The thought of joining them crossed our minds, but how could we play with the neighbourhood kids if we didn't understand their language? We stayed inside and assumed the role of spectators. We spent all our Saturdays watching other kids play on the television screen, or out the window. Fearing as well as longing for the world outside.

The television wasn't merely our smokescreen; it was also our babysitter, our daycare worker, and our only friend. We spent hours in its company. *Passe-Partout* taught us the basics of the French language better than any other program. Repeating *un oiseau** five hundred times will have that effect. Over the following years, I listened to each of the show's episodes religiously, even after having learned the language. When I was eleven, even twelve, I still sat there out of nostalgia, the lights dimmed, as if at Mass, in communion with the other little Québécois kids, watching somersaults and little dramas. I comforted myself with these moments; it was like visiting a place where I belonged.

---

* A bird.

But that morning, we didn't move, didn't say a word, just stayed there for a long time watching a snowball fight. It was an excruciatingly painful, magnificent show, the snow dancing around in the air to the kids' shrieks and laughter. We knew we were outsiders, shut-ins, excluded from their play. We were stuck in this domestic sphere, understanding nothing, not even the simple words from the Little Beaver's theme song.

It wasn't fair how alive it was outside without us.

That morning, my brother and I got our revenge. We made up our own language.

Alessona soon became one of the words in the new language that my little brother and I conjured up. It didn't mean anything; it was just a familiar series of syllables we could repeat. The real world eluded us, relegated us to silence, to the impossibility of communicating, and our only revenge was to pretend to have a language that only we understood. We chose to withdraw from a world that refused us access rather than try to make it our own.

Nothing frightened us more than the sounds from the nearby alley. We couldn't understand anything that was said. The social codes were even more obscure. There were endless cries of "Arrêêête Kevin"* and "Geneviève, viens dîner tusuite!"† We had no wish to confront this reality. Instead, we thought that with three or four little twigs we could build a castle, a castle we hoped would protect us.

We had a hilarious time with onomatopes, syllables, and words. Except we weren't saying anything. Because language is collective, and we were all alone.

For several weeks, we pretended to ignore the constant babbling of the other kids, and instead focused on our own new invented sounds. At least until I went to the welcome class. Once I began to sample the common language, I'd leave all the *alessonas*, like the burden of having five mouths to feed, to my parents.

---

* "Stop it, Kevin!"
† "Genevieve, come eat your lunch right now!"

A polar bear on the bus[18]

IT WAS A SUNNY BUT GLACIAL WINTER AFTERNOON. OUR family was out together, despite the cold. This was pretty rare, so we were all supercharged. As we waited for the bus that would take us to *la Fête des neiges*,* we hopped up and down with impatience on the sidewalk of Sauvé Street. Our parents let us goof around in line despite the disapproving glances from some of the ladies in their Sunday best. Playing outside in the winter was not a thing we did—and it still isn't. Year after year, we spent the end of November to the beginning of April inside, repressing our energy or letting it loose once in a while, during trips to Super Carnaval,[19] behind the big Rossy[20] store, or in the empty parking lots of the banks my parents cleaned.

My parents had two jobs each, three children, debts coming out of their ears, and family to send money to back in Chile. So they scrimped and saved and used every trick imaginable to save

---

* The Snow Festival.

a few dollars. They'd found a good little scam that allowed them to save on transit: taking turns using a single bus pass. Since there were no ticket inspectors, the first one to board the bus showed the pass to the driver. Then they went and sat in the back, opened the window, and threw the card to the other person. That person waited for the next bus to come and—technically, without breaking the law—presented the same pass to the driver. This was before electronic ticket scanners and STM[21] inspections on youths, cheaters, and poor people.

When the bus finally arrived, my father decided to get on first with *los chicos*,* as he called my little brother and me. My mother would stay at the metro exit with my older brother, who already had a student pass, and they would wait there, freezing, until the next bus came. My little brother and I charged to the back of the bus like a couple of feral urchins, pushing and shoving our way past people. My father apologized for us, although our behaviour actually suited his purposes; we always managed to get seats at the back of the bus. He'd walk toward us with a serious, reproachful expression on his face and then casually open the window on the right side and shout goodbye to my mother. My little brother and I just wordlessly waved at the window before quickly looking away. Even though they'd never explained it to us, we knew that our parents cheated, how they did it, but especially why they did it. When necessary, we looked the other way.

The bus left. I don't remember the journey, just that when we arrived, we had to wait fifteen minutes before we caught sight of the next bus, the one my mother and brother were supposed to catch to meet us. The wait was cold, long, and boring, almost unbearable for children, but it was the price we paid for having just one monthly pass. When the next bus finally appeared, the rest of my family wasn't on it. Nor were they on the one after that, which seemed to take three centuries to arrive.

---

* The children.

My father tried to hide his alarm, but we saw his frown, his hand-wringing, and something off about his smile. I also remember the anxiety I had no words for but that whirled around in a loop inside my head: *My mother's been caught, the bus police have brought her to the STM prison, they're going to deport us.* I was a prisoner of my rumination while my father kept checking his watch. After forty minutes of being frozen with dread, we finally spotted my mother running toward us. She was anxious and out of breath, her face red with shame and effort.

My dad's shaking voice betrayed the acute panic he'd been repressing in front of us. "*¿Te vieron?*"*

No. They hadn't been caught cheating. It was just that my father had thrown the bus pass at the last minute, when the bus had already started moving. The pass had landed between the window and an ad on the bus and had gotten stuck there. My older brother and my mother had seen the bus, insensible to the unfolding drama, pull away. With no pass and no money, they'd walked the whole way, like a couple of wretches. My frustrated father kept badgering my mother with questions: Why didn't you run after the bus? Why didn't you wave? Why didn't you shout? My exhausted mother howled back: they *had* shouted and waved, but we hadn't seen or heard anything.

I don't know how long they yelled at each other; I was slumped, immobile, on my little bench, at once terrified, relieved, and annoyed. *It's all right, we can stay, we won't be deported, nobody figured out our scam,* but also, *It's the end of the month, we can't buy another pass. We're going to have to pay for the remaining days one at a time.* I made calculations and budgets in silence: *That'll cost an arm and a leg, how are we going to pay for all the commutes, can my parents afford two bus passes?*

Without my noticing, they'd stopped arguing and had begun to walk. We went to *la Fête des neiges,* but our hearts weren't in it anymore.

---

* "They saw you?"

The surprise in the cereal box

THERE WERE SEVENTEEN OF US KIDS, EACH A DIFFERENT shade. Well, all the shades of people that are called "visible minorities." No white people in the class, apart from the teacher.

We had to unlearn our habit of calling her Miss Teacher, as we did in our respective countries. In fact, she had no last name. It must have been something that the little refugee I was found impossible to write or pronounce correctly. Something like Beaulieu, Ouellet, or Gaudreault. For us immigrant kids in the welcome class at École La Visitation near Henri-Bourassa, her name was Madame Thérèse.

Madame Thérèse was old. I mean, I think she was, because she was wrinkled, elegantly dressed, and had the nonchalance of one who has practised her profession for a hundred years. She never seemed worried and, articulating carefully, rolling her Rs as you were supposed to, often told us: "You will learn French. *Ce n'est pas si sorcier.** You'll see." I repeated her words to myself. I translated

---

* "It's not exactly witchcraft," i.e., it's not hard.

them but couldn't really understand what she was talking about. What did this have to do with sorcery? Comprehension would come. In the meantime, her words were slow and loud, as if we were hard of hearing. I liked her reassuring presence.

I don't think I made any friends in Madame Thérèse's class. We all had the same wide, frightened eyes, and we were all trying to learn the necessary codes to get through the day, to ask where the bathrooms were, to say, *I lost my scarf, I miss my mother.* To survive the beginning of 1987. No friendships yet. Get to know our new environment. I remember the violence of the wind in February, followed by brown slush in March. What *is* that? Half-frozen mud?

I remember being numb with cold. Wet boots, damp socks, smelly feet. One thing I know is that we were learning to embrace winter at the same time as we learned the French words for blowing snow and freezing rain. "'*Stie qu'y fait frette*"* would come later, when my parents had the money to move into an apartment big enough for all five of us in Hochelaga. For the moment, in our badly insulated little four-and-a-half in Ahuntsic, we could talk about snowflakes, frost, and polar bears.

It was always warm in Madame Thérèse's classroom. It was dry and noisy. I don't know if we succeeded in communicating with our multiple mother tongues and the three hundred or so French words we each had, but it seems to me we were always talking. What on earth could we have been talking about? Probably "*J'ai froid*" or "*Il fait froid*"† ad nauseum. Shivering together against the cold windows in the north of the city. Sharing what we could: our sense of how cold it was. We didn't have much in common. I was Latina; there were Turks, a North African, a Kurd. We weren't yet Québécois. Not even close. I didn't know where the others were from and, honestly, it really didn't matter. Because we all had cheeks reddened by winter and a family story of exile we never talked about.

---

* "Fuck, is it cold!"
† "I'm cold"; "It's cold."

Madame Thérèse certainly had some rather curious teaching methods, but we couldn't really criticize her as we *were* learning French pretty quickly. Even the Chinese kids managed to learn French in her class—as I told my parents in Spanish. I was so impressed: even the Chinese kids! As for me, I sat between the Kurdish boy and a Turkish girl and forced myself to understand the new words and to repeat them.

My time in Madame Thérèse's class for non-francophone immigrants was a significantly arduous chapter of my life. Yet besides the glacial temperatures and the dryness, I've only retained one memory.

Madame Thérèse liked to test our knowledge and evaluate our progress. We had tons of words to absorb. We needed to memorize them every evening after school. "*Traîneau, pelleter, banc de neige.*"* We had to hurry up; spring was coming. To motivate us, she brought a huge box of Honeycomb cereal. A huge, Costco-sized, beautiful, bright red box. The pieces of cereal looked like flowers, I thought. It was only years later that I understood what they were supposed to represent. It had been such a long time since I'd seen flowers.

We'd get hungry, but our teacher made us wait. She'd spend a good minute looking through her cards to find one at the right level—difficult enough to represent a challenge, but not to the extent that we would feel discouraged. She went and got the box—so slowly that it was excruciating for us. She put it on her desk, the top wide open, then started her quiz.

First, she'd choose a kid who was *not* super keen and pick one of hundreds of illustrations from her plasticized cards. Everyone had a turn; we each had to associate a word or expression with the picture. If we succeeded, she gave us a handful of cereal from her gigantic box. No milk, just the sweet cereal. From her mani-cured, ring-adorned hand to our chubby little fists with our dirty fingernails.

---

* "Sled, shovelling, snowbank."

It was the end of February, and there was a snowstorm. The Chinese girl—who was almost certainly Korean—was chosen first. An illustration of shoes with blades. She said, "*Patins.*"* Easy. She got some cereal. She made a lot of noise as she ate, which made it harder to concentrate. I told myself: as long as I get to go soon. Madame Thérèse picked the Kurdish boy. The picture depicted three white balls, arranged vertically, topped with a bowler hat, and a carrot where its nose would be. He took his time, bit his lip, and said, "*Homme à neige.*"† I knew that that wasn't exactly it. The teacher probably thought something like, "Well, almost." She corrected him: "*Bonhomme de neige,*"‡ articulating "*Bo-nho-mme.*" He started to get anxious; his eyes never left the box of cereal. He repeated, "*Bonhomme de neige.*" The Kurdish boy, who didn't have a country, was allowed to get a handful of Honeycombs for his almost *bonhomme de neige.*

It was my turn. My hands were sweaty, my mouth tight, my stomach keen, and I had to pee. I watched her go through her cards, pout, shake her head. Rejecting any that were too obvious, considering the more difficult ones. Choosing one just for me. She showed it to me: a man going down a hill with sticks under his boots. Shit, it was a sport. A winter sport. I didn't know anything about winter sports. Before coming to Québec, I hadn't even known there were Winter Olympics.

"Ski?"

She looked at me, raised an eyebrow, and waited. She knew I was capable of giving her a more precise answer.

"Ski...*ski alpin!*"§ Ah! I did it! "*Ski alpin,*" I repeated with pride, following this with a hearty, victorious laugh. When I went to get my handful of Honeycombs, she asked me if I'd ever done any downhill skiing. I'd just memorized the drawing, it wasn't *sorcier.*

---

* "Skates."

† "Man of snow."

‡ "Snowman."

§ "Downhill skiing."

I didn't know at the time that thirty winters would go by and my answer would still be the same. No, Madame Thérèse, I've never gone downhill skiing. It's not your fault, it's just that it's not really our thing. How did she always find the most challenging picture for each of us? She managed every single time. Anyway, all seventeen children in the welcome class gained some weight during this period. We experienced winter and learned French, one bite of cereal at a time. I guess that's what they call learning by heart.

Today, Honeycomb cereal makes me feel too emotional; I never buy it. It tastes sweetly of honey but also the glacial uncertainty of our first days in a northern country. Even just smelling it brings that time back. The smell of sugar. Of *I can't understand anything*. Of the *Where the hell are we?* that claws at the stomachs of all uprooted children. And the damp felt from dozens of little boots that dry for hours on the classroom heater in Madame Thérèse's classroom.

PART II

The fact that only the son speaks and only him is a violent thing for both of them: the father is deprived of the possibility of telling the story of his own life and the son would like to have a response that he will never obtain.
—Édouard Louis

Au clair de la lune[22]

I DIDN'T USE TO CARE. I USED TO BE AUDACIOUS, COURAGEOUS, intrepid, and wild. I wasn't even the slightest bit familiar with fear. I climbed trees, found it hilarious if anyone could see my underwear, I stuck my tongue out, defied all authority that struck me as illegitimate, I spoke in a loud voice, and I loved all the boys around me, especially my big brother.

When I was three years old, my brother, at the grand old age of ten, was my hero and role model. He'd leave every morning, walking up the dirt road—there were no sidewalks. I watched as he climbed a steep hill to get to his school, the same school where my father taught English. They walked up slowly, for long minutes. My brother sometimes skipping a bit, or other times kicking pebbles like a condemned prisoner, my father always patient. I'd watch them until they gradually slipped from my envious gaze. They were outside, dressed in their uniforms for the occasion—jacket, tie, dress pants—whereas I stayed home in my mismatched pyjamas with my aunt, my grandmother, my mother, and my baby brother, an infant who had not yet learned to walk. This is where I grew bored, between the household chores and these sighing, aproned women who waited for the days to begin and end, never leaving a trace of themselves anywhere, a dishcloth always in their hands, wiping away any fingerprints they came across as they moved from the kitchen to the living room.

They were trapped in an endless cycle of scrimping and saving, writing grocery lists, cooking meals, washing dishes, drying them, putting them away, dealing with leftovers, washing clothes, hanging sheets on the line, folding underwear, socks, comforters, picking up everyone else's trash. Hearing the radio murmur of the outside world, changing diapers, treating bumps and bruises, tickling babies, and, in the best cases, listening to the local gossip, repeated ad nauseum by the lovable neighbour whom everyone called the Crackpot. I wanted to get off that incessant domestic merry-go-round, escape the house's suffocating embrace. I longed to take the dirt road, climb up the hill, learn to read, write, and count.

I was three years old, and I got it into my head that I absolutely had to get out, had to face the challenge of school. I asked—even demanded—that they sign me up every single day, many times a day, for weeks that turned into months. My poor mother, listening to my litany, tried to occupy me as well as she could, but little Caroline, overcome with frustration, was insistent and persuasive. I never let up, and "I wanna go to school too" quickly became the first thing I said in the morning, my eyes still blurry from night, and the last thing I said before going to bed. My parents were not the kind who would just yield to my whims, but "I wanna go to school too" soon became my personal catchphrase, almost a character trait.

After I'd relentlessly pestered my father, my brother, my mother, my aunt, and my grandmother, as well as the Crackpot, my parents finally decided to give in. My father took the necessary steps at his workplace to have me enrolled. Like me, he had to push. They weren't going to just let in a three-year-old girl without a show of resistance. However, this was Chile in the eighties, and there were ways around the bureaucracy. My father had been on staff for a long time; he was well-liked, involved, kind of a big shot. With a bit of administrative smoke and mirrors, they finally got me into kindergarten. So there I was, three and a quarter years old, officially an elementary school pupil.

My parents didn't bet a cent on my finishing the year, not because the program was too difficult for me, but rather because of my little body's capacity to keep up with kids twice my age. But they also knew my pigheadedness and pride would push me to give it all I had.

Kids from kindergarten to the end of high school shared the same building. At three years old, I was literally the smallest person attending school. So tiny, in fact, that my parents had to have a seamstress sew me a uniform, still obligatory in Chilean schools. I quickly became the school mascot, a little two-legged thing that whirred around with an outsize schoolbag in the yard, hanging out with fifteen- and sixteen-year-olds as if this was perfectly normal. I felt very much at home.

Saying I loved school is an understatement. I'd found a place where so much was possible! It managed to break the monotony I'd found so dispiriting. The ennui I'd been trying to repress for months finally dissipated. School welcomed my overflowing personality, and I thrived there; I was the best I could be. I was finally occupied and challenged, no longer held back and hemmed in. I'd been aching to go to school, and as soon as I set foot inside, I knew school would always be both my playground and ultimate destination. I came home completely drained, it's true. But I adored everything: the routine, learning stuff, playtime, the scents of sharpened pencils, of chalk, the noise of desks being moved, the excitement before the bell rang, the schoolyard dramas, the variety of perspectives I encountered. I liked all but one thing, and that's what killed my school year: being told what to do, and the obedience and domination that implied.

I just could not deal with that, and the day we fingerpainted, I became a three-year-old dropout.

And yet it was one of my favourite activities. They gave us each a palette with three holes. Which meant we had to choose three colours.

I chose red, three times.

"That's not three colours," the teacher said.

"Yes, it is. It's red, red, and red."

"Caroline, in a couple of minutes you're going to be asking me for other colours."

"No, I just want a lot of red."

She sighed. I saw the weariness in her expression. She let me have my three reds before going off to deal with another child, who was whining because she wanted a fourth colour. The teacher refused, of course, but the little girl started arguing, and also asking other children around her if she could have their palettes, to complete the rainbow she was painting. In vain.

I watched her. I knew she was a bit cheeky and that she'd be coming around in no time to get some of my red paint, a colour she didn't have. I saw her eyes light up: the teacher had left the big jar of yellow paint a few centimetres away from me. I confess that it was tempting.

The little girl leaned furtively toward me and whispered in my ear: "Pass me the yellow." I refused, of course. I might have been three years younger than her, but I wasn't stupid. Everyone knows that teachers have eyes on the backs of their heads, and there was no way I was going to get told off for an amateur stunt like that. She persisted: "If you do it really fast, she won't see us." I shook my head, looked away, and focused on my work of art. The little girl would not stop fidgeting on her chair. She finally decided to go for it herself. She suddenly flung out her arm to grab the jar of paint. Except she was a few millimetres too far away and her clumsy fingers barely made contact—just enough to knock it over. The cap hadn't been screwed on tightly, and the enormous bottle lost it in mid-flight, allowing the yellow paint to splatter its ignominy everywhere. First on the table, then all over the floor, splashing the walls as it went, the chair legs, our navy-blue pants.

The teacher turned around, saw the treacherous spray of paint. It seemed to have started its journey right next to me.

"Caroline!"

"It wasn't me, miss."

She knew that I could be troublesome, even rude, but not dishonest. "Who was it then?"

I lowered my eyes.

A constellation of yellow stars sprinkled my earth-coloured shoes. It was beautiful, incongruous. I hesitated. I didn't particularly like that little girl. In fact, I found her irritating, but that wasn't a reason to squeal on a classmate.

"I can't tell you, miss."

"That's what I thought. You're going to have to go sit in the corner, Caroline."

"No! It's not fair! It wasn't me!"

"Who was it then?"

"I DON'T WANT TO TELL YOU!"

Her shoulders slumped. It was the end of the day and everything about her exuded discouragement and fatigue. She could have wiped this away with a sponge, but she just looked at the ground, and at her own shoes, splattered with yellow drops. Her pantyhose too, her last pair without any runs.

"Caroline, go sit in the corner."

This time, I looked her in the eyes. "NO. It wasn't me. I'm not going to tell you who it was, and I'm not going to sit in the corner."

So obviously, I ended up in the corner, mortified and sulking. As I looked around the beige classroom, I noticed how dirty the walls were, how the paint was peeling. And despite my enthusiasm for school, and the delight I felt every day when I arrived, I made the decision not to return. I didn't say anything about this to the teacher. When the bell announced the end of my humiliation, I got my bag, filled it with my possessions, and went outside, my mood more bitter than morose. I didn't look back.

As if all of this hadn't been enough, it started to rain as I walked home. Despite my umbrella, the drops drummed down on my shoes, making the paint run and gradually slide off my feet onto the muddy ground. An array of little yellow splotches all the way home.

Once home, I hung up my bag for the last time and announced my decision to my parents. The next day, and all the days that followed, I would refuse to return to school. But at dusk that evening, standing at my window by the light of the moon, I looked at the little sunny spots on the newly dry ground. With my mother's comforting bustle in the background as a kind of soundtrack, I looked at them, all shiny and yellow. My mother noticed me staring out the window and left the dishes to come stand at my side. For long minutes she too gazed out at my brilliant, stellar route. Without saying a word, she laid a gentle hand on my shoulder. And I smiled without reserve—proud, dignified, and satisfied.

My Little Julie[23]

HALFWAY THROUGH 1987, THE WELCOME CLASS WOULD BE nothing more to me than a collection of vague impressions. No more faces: they all died in the little refugee's vault like those of people we have no photos of and can't remember anymore. Like my memory of Chile, foggy recollections.

I'd spent a winter in the protective bubble of the Canadian multicultural mosaic fantasyland that was the *classe de francization*.* I'd passed the first phase of becoming a super model of successful integration: I was accepted into the regular program. However, in the schoolyard of École primaire Louis-Colin in Ahuntsic, it felt like I was crossing a threshold into a new country once again. There weren't a lot of immigrants at this school, and if there were any, they were mostly white, which wasn't the same thing. I couldn't melt into the crowd like before: I stuck out.

---

* French language and culture class.

On those first days, I couldn't tell the other kids apart; all the little girls looked identical to me. Very nice, very healthy, quiet, boring. Dozens of Julies, slim, dressed in pale colours, pink smiles, vaguely pleasant-looking, fine blond hair. Some said their hair was light brown, but if there was a difference, I couldn't tell, and, frankly, it seemed exaggerated. And they called any colour beyond dark brown "black."

I started Grade 2 with my thick black braids that rarely held for a whole day, my extra pounds from my daily *pancito*,* my denim overalls, which only I thought were cool, my old washed-out florescent pink T-shirt or the purple jogging suit bought at a liquidation sale at Woolworth's, and my white recorder. A recorder in my pocket—as if I was above social conventions.

All of this may have bolstered my qualities of independence and originality had I not been so conscious of my misfit status. And maybe also if this hadn't been communicated to me with a certain scorn, which I'd later understand carried a sense of superiority mixed with disdain and pity. "Your mother didn't do your hair this morning?" they'd ask me as they carefully removed their pink balaclavas to free their smooth hair, a barrette on one side, and I took off my staticky brown hand-knit *tuque*, messing up my own hair. I talked with my hands, I had an accent and a loud voice, I played the fucking flute. I was outrageously enthusiastic, noisy, loud. My *whole being* was loud next to these girls, whom I found so delicate in the privilege of their anonymity.

I could never be enough of a chameleon to look like them, so it was my personality that had to go. At eight years old, I decided to avoid standing out from the crowd. I practised talking without my hands in the mirror. I hid my excitement in class. I learned not to laugh too loud at the other girls' jokes. I forced myself to walk rather than run at recess. This self-restraint came to define my social persona. If I couldn't turn off the little Latina in me, I'd at least have done my best to diminish her through a campaign of

---

* Bread roll.

gradual extinction. By toning down my colours and curbing my enthusiasm, I created a sort of muffled childhood for myself.

At the same time, everything screamed that I'd never be a little Julie. When I was asked my name and I proudly answered, "Caroline," without an accent, because I'd practised it as if I were training for an Olympic event, there was always an uncomfortable pause that betrayed my listener's skepticism, whether they were an adult or a child. The Julies of my school, no fools, invariably ended up asking, "Caroline? Are you adopted?"

No, I answered, sheepish and embarrassed. I never had the time to tell them that my father had been an English teacher in Chile and that he and my mother had chosen English names for each of their three children. Their disinterest immediately appeared on their faces and, as I was erased, I watched them withdraw; I went back to the suffocating silence of a life without echoes, of subdued oscillations and muted disquiet.

Shit-eaters[24]

LIKE ALL THE OTHER LUNCH BOXES OF THAT TIME, MINE WAS rectangular, made of hard plastic, and composed of two compartments. Its bright shade of canary yellow slowly faded as the school year ground on. I liked to place it horizontally on the old white Formica folding table, the kind typically found in Montreal's public elementary schools. A small burst of happiness seized me every time I placed it there. I was a chubby kid who loved to eat. Every time I entered the tiny neon-lit cafeteria, no matter the neighbourhood and no matter the school, the same expectation, mixed with agitation, tugged at my stomach.

I was starving, eager to taste my food, but I contemplated my little yellow box for a long time and with a certain amount of fear before opening it. My apprehension began to torment me once I set it in front of me at the edge of the table. The moment I opened it, the pinching began in my stomach. Would I be able to eat in peace? Was my lunch going to attract stares? Would it look weird? Would it smell strange? We weren't Québécois; we didn't have thermoses.

It would never occur to my mother to buy one, nor to me to ask for one. Anyway, I'd already told my mother not to pack hot lunches for me, since they always smelled stronger than cold ones.

That day, impatient and nervous, I didn't feel like prolonging the ordeal. Excited but watchful, I snapped open my box. Damn, a sandwich with *dulce de leche*.* No one had heard of that in 1988. I ate it every week, but I'd never seen or heard of it anywhere but at home. Actually, in Chile, we used to call it *manjar*,† and here in Québec, I didn't have any French words to name what I ate.

"Hey, do you see that? She's got this weird peanut butter."

"It's not peanut butter. It's called *manjar*, it's like caram—"

"It looks like shit."

Another one for my list of foods to be eaten in secret. The day before, it had been *pan con palta*. In the eighties, nobody Instagrammed their slices of avocado toast, and the sidelong glances I got from other kids at my table soon convinced me to keep my *pan con palta* out of view as much as possible. I left them in my lunchbox. I'd wolf them down, out of sight of the other kids, when I got home, where it was sociably acceptable to enjoy what the others called vomit bread.

This time I was too hungry, I couldn't wait until evening. I devoured my slices of bread with the homemade *manjar* without even tasting its sweetness. I swallowed my bread and my shame in such a hurry I gave myself the hiccups. It got stuck in my throat. Between each hiccup that shook my little body, I tasted the bitterness of being different.

Even if I tried to reason with myself, repeating that the real *mangeux de marde*‡ were the little cops who terrorized me in the cafeteria, I knew I couldn't take being terrified every single day at noon. So I used the only means available to me.

---

*   A spreadable, creamy caramel-like sauce.

†   Delicacy.

‡   Shit-eaters.

"*Mamá*, I don't want you to put any *manjar* or *palta** in my lunches."

"*¿Por que?*"†

"I don't like it anymore."

As an immigrant child, the only way I could fit in was by being ashamed of who I was, rejecting what I was made of. A series of small betrayals of myself and of my parents. I learned to exist only through the eyes of others, trying to anticipate their reactions. I was eight years old and I'd already forbidden my mother to pack anything that could be seen as exotic in my lunches, thereby alienating myself from my culture of origin. Leading the battle all the way to what was on my plate every lunch break constituted my biggest challenge at school; I surrendered by depriving myself of what I enjoyed, giving up little bits of me.

"I don't like it anymore." The first in a long series of lies I told as I learned to be something like a real Québécoise.

---

*   Avocado.

†   "Why?"

Working's too hard[25]

SHE'D WORKED IN A DAYCARE BACK IN CHILE. SHE'D ALSO done children's theatre. She laughed constantly; she spread joy and wonder wherever she went. He taught English and worked for the union. He used to be the one everyone watched and listened to. But here my parents had lives that consisted of taking orders, staying silent, avoiding eye contact. Over the years, they were forced to take on a countless number of crappy, exhausting jobs to keep our family alive. Among these was cleaning offices in a bank at night. My parents worked incognito, with no one looking at them. When the offices were closed, when it was dark out, when it was quiet.

It was too dim for anyone to see that my mother was one of those people who adored little kids, even those who weren't hers. And she'd spend her whole life kicking herself for having missed a great chunk of our childhoods while working two or three jobs to survive. No one would guess that my father was the best orator I've ever met, that when he spoke, everyone listened. When he cleaned, he clammed up.

Every night after school, they hauled us along to one of the branches of the CIBC,[26] where we kept them company as they cleaned the offices. They had to moonlight, but at least we were together.

Which pissed me off.

My boredom was nothing compared to what my parents had to go through, wiping the toilets of about twenty employees. I'd whine because I was so bored while my mother had her head in a toilet bowl and my father destroyed his back vacuuming two floors of the building. Sweat ran down their bodies while my little brother and I pretended to draw in the stark, empty lunchroom. A room that smelled of the dirty coffee machine filter, the plastic of the water coolers with their 18.9-litre containers, and a mix of Windex and bleach.

We weren't allowed to touch anything, so we touched everything when no one was looking. The high we got from discovering things would last a week or two. At first, we explored the whole area without moving anything out of place. Then we gradually started to make ourselves at home. We sat on the chairs, opened drawers. We quickly found the candy, tampons, and condoms. We went through people's appointment diaries, read all the pieces of paper we found, even the ones in the garbage. We inspected everything, absolutely everything. My parents worked, and we kept ourselves busy. So much so that when it was over, I knew everything about the life and habits of all the employees. Like a detective, I examined all the hints I found about other people's lives.

That's where I learned to make sense of my world—by looking at the scraps of information that the day people left behind. The people who lived sunlit lives and who enjoyed full citizenship here. It's where I learned to give meaning to the sparse fragments they left behind, even when those fragments ended up in the garbage. I learned to live vicariously.

Among the twenty or so employees working at that branch of the CIBC, Madame Cyr was the one who affected me most. After she'd been absent for a few days, and there was nothing to clean in her cubicle, I came across the photograph of her husband that had previously occupied a prominent place on her desk. It was out of its plastic frame, torn in half, in the garbage.

I fished it out.

In fact, I didn't merely fish it out. I fished it out and stuck the two halves back together, using Madame Cyr's own Scotch tape. I wanted to keep it and wait six months, a year, whatever time it took for the necessary water to flow under the bridge. I wanted to wait until the divorce had been settled and absorbed before putting it back among her things. To revive the memories once the anger had subsided. I'd planned to keep it and sneak it back between the pages of a Danielle Steel book she'd left lying on the corner of her desk. A bookmark. She might have suspected a colleague with ill intentions, not a little eight-year-old refugee dying of boredom while her parents worked themselves to death.

Did anyone know of our existence? I made sure they did. Even if it was out of the question for me to leave my name at the scene of the crime, I wanted to leave some sort of trace. I didn't want to remain invisible. But well, I was eight years old, so of course I ended up losing that picture. And then the photo of her and her kids on vacation—which came to replace the one of their father—was really nice. Madame Cyr had cut her hair and changed her glasses. She looked looser, with a frank sort of smile, despite her sad eyes.

And then there was the boss. Or an assistant boss, the kind who still has to work for real. He had the biggest office, one of the only ones with a window, and a gigantic bookcase my mother hated. It held only economics textbooks and binders filled with financial regulations that took too long to dust. No real books. Not one, not even a Danielle Steel. The assistant boss was the only one who didn't have a regular chair. He had an armchair. A leather armchair that swivelled. I loved to spend time in that too-big armchair and look at the bookcase empty of real books. I didn't want his job, but I wanted to be in his spot.

It was in that chair, the one that belonged to that CIBC assistant boss in the late eighties, that I got the idea of writing a book.

If we had to be there every day of the week, I might as well filch a few legal-size sheets of paper, fold them, and staple them together to make a book.

So, my first book. A bestseller with a print run of one single copy. I wrote the story, and my little brother helped me illustrate it. It recounted the odyssey of two children who find all kinds of excuses to get out of cleaning their room. Page after page of how they succeed in avoiding their mess and let someone else deal with it.

The book was entitled *Housework Is Ridiculous*, but it could just as well have been called *The Great Disavowal*. Our betrayal was not exactly subtle; it could not have been clearer. While our parents wore themselves out trying to put bread on the table—our table—we disassociated ourselves from them to give vent to our ennui.

When I think about the work my parents did in those days, what strikes me is that it never occurred to us to help them. And they never asked us to.

Our entire youth, my parents worked themselves to the bone cleaning up after other people. Rich people in their big houses on Nuns' Island, luxury apartments in Westmount, five-star hotels downtown, dentists' offices on the South Shore, banks with glass walls and chilly architecture like the CIBC building. They cleaned up after other people so that those other people had the luxury of being bored. Our creative process was born there, in the bottom of garbage cans our parents emptied so that we could sit quietly, observing the world and putting it into words.

Le Bonhomme Carnaval[27]

BY GRADE 3, I'D ATTENDED THREE ELEMENTARY SCHOOLS: I was now on my fourth. After the one in Chile, the welcome class, and the regular school, I attended one that was not part of the Catholic School Board. Instead of religion, my Protestant school provided more instruction in English, something the language teacher who still lived inside my father's body found really important. École Ahuntsic was at the edge of the city, facing a never-ending line of speeding cars on Saint-Laurent.

I was quiet and watchful like my only two friends, pleasant little girls, content, without any great ambitions. I was careful to be co-operative, avoid making waves, and never respond to the name-calling, to the soft violence that children inflict on other children, and that escapes the notice of adults. I'd been around the block. My formerly loud, boisterous, tree-climbing, rough-around-the-edges personality had been smoothed and polished through a process of slow attrition, from contact with this new culture.

I was quite keen to go to school; I didn't whine about it. I liked to sit in class and listen to the teacher. To try to keep up in class, constantly prove to her I could. Do well at school without drawing attention to myself. Be good enough while never actually outshining anyone. I had become a perfect little girl who raised her hand, waited her turn, was never disruptive in class; I'd become what was expected of me.

On the weekends, sick of TV, I'd take out my school supplies to entertain myself. I'd colour, draw, use my little plastic ruler to measure things, make circles with my compass, learn dictations by heart, but more than anything else, I'd write. I'd keep myself frantically busy writing songs and poems. I would have done that my whole life, be a poet, had I known such a thing was possible.

There was one poem I was particularly proud of: "My Snowman." Nothing happened; I just described a snowman. In the process, by appropriating winter, I finally accepted and embraced it. I worked on that poem for weeks. Started over, erased, rewrote, searching for the exact words, the precise tone. I pared it down, playing with the sounds, trying to find its music. And when I had finished rewriting it, after three Saturdays' worth of TV cartoons, I found it perfect. Every word had been painstakingly considered, not one was unnecessary. I wanted to honour it; I carefully wrote it over like a scribe from the Middle Ages, with my best calligraphy. This was in the notebook I'd stolen from one of the desks at the bank where my parents worked.

I was embellishing the title with snowflakes when I heard my father get up. I obeyed my instinct, which was to hide the notebook. Too late—the frantic movement betrayed me, aroused my dad's suspicion. Before he could scold me, I said, "It's my poem," hoping to distract him from my crime. Surprised, he held out his hand to read it. I gave him the stolen notebook with trepidation and waited, watching his eyes go from surprise to incredulity. I was so scared of being scolded that I closed my eyes until he asked me, in an amazed voice, "*¿Tú lo escribiste?*" * He didn't wait for me to

---

* "You wrote that?"

answer. "¡*Muestralo a Madame Monique! Llévatelo al colegio mañana y muestralo a tu profe.*" *

It blew my mind: I'd impressed my father and hadn't even been told off for my theft. I spent a good part of the afternoon transcribing the poem on a sheet of lined paper.

I didn't want to push my luck. I savoured all the words as I recopied them, confident that these words were the right ones. Once I'd finished, I filled the margins with decorative flourishes. I would have liked to add a lovely snowman, but my artistic talent was a bit limited and I didn't want to mess up my poem with childish scribbles. So I copied a Bonhomme Carnaval from a brochure I'd found in our junk mail. I had no idea that it had been the Québec Carnaval's emblem for thirty years. Looking over my work, now adorned with an attractive, deeply original snowman with what I thought was a scarf around his waist, I felt a rush of pride: my beautiful, musical poem now also had some colour.

I was trembling and excited on Monday morning. I'd woken up at dawn and rehearsed what I'd say to Madame Monique all morning. But once I got to school, I was too nervous. My stomach was in knots until noon as I waited for the right moment to talk to her. Lunchtime gave me some time to laugh and relax with my friends and get up the courage to go and see her. As I returned to class, in a little voice that apologized for existing, I said, "Excuse me for bothering you, Madame Monique, may I give you a poem I wrote? I think it's pretty good. My father even told me to show it to you."

I remember everything: her intrigued face, her wrinkled hand as it delicately moved a strand of greying hair behind her ear before taking the sheet I anxiously offered her, her furtive brown eyes as they quickly skimmed over my words. And her drawer. Her desk drawer, the obscure hole into which she casually threw my sheet. "I'll look at it this week when I have time, okay?"

---

* "Show it to Madame Monique! Bring it to school tomorrow and show it to your teacher."

I watched every move she made, all week long. I couldn't stop looking in her direction. Unable to concentrate, I scrutinized her comings and goings: from her desk to the board and from the board back to her desk. She never once opened her drawer, and this managed to enhance both its mystery and significance for me. I figured it contained whatever she considered to be most important and precious. I told myself that she was undoubtedly waiting for the weekend to read my poem in the quiet of her apartment.

I imagined her in the same way that I did all the women I considered upper-class: dressed in black, in high heels, a glass of white wine in her hand, in a very clean house full of old books and shag carpets. She would read my poem Sunday night in her leather armchair by the fireplace and return to class the next day with photocopies for everyone. She'd congratulate me, and then read my poem out loud in a ceremonious voice while the other kids sat in silent amazement at being witness to my apparent transformation from a silent, bashful little refugee to a girl who brilliantly tinkered with grammar and turned it into poetry. These words, my words, would be heard.

Monday arrived and she said nothing, not a word about my snowman all day long. I came home confused, defeated, and sullen. I barely slept all night, trying to make sense of her silence. Hadn't she liked it? Had she found it so awful that she didn't want to talk about it? Could it be that terrible? The next day I went to see her, intimidated, my stomach in knots, my frightened little face broadcasting my dread.

"Madame Monique, did you have time to read my poem?"

"What poem?"

A dark cloud of frustration fogged up my eyes. I bit my lip. I don't know what words or tone I used to remind her of my poem, her promise, her drawer, but she opened it. Way back, buried under little wooden pencil stubs, there it was, all wrinkled up. You could see Bonhomme Carnaval's foolish grin poking out.

"Oh, that. Uh, no. But I will—when I get the time."

The verdict had come down, even before she'd read a single word. She'd decided it couldn't possibly be interesting. The poem lay there, crumpled and forgotten among store receipts, plastic forks, old stencils, capless pens, and tiny, useless pencils. My poem was deemed only good enough for the junk drawer, where it would disappear amid other detritus. I realized she would never read it. She'd condemned it before even doing so. In her eyes, I didn't exist. All I'd succeeded in doing by becoming a reserved, obedient, docile, and quiet child was to render myself completely invisible.

I spent the rest of the year actively despising Madame Monique, mentally tallying everything I would not be, with her as the main counter-model. I'd add others to that list as time went by, and while I certainly wasn't ready to raise my voice, I already knew for sure that it was out of this seething resentment that little Caroline, whom I'd buried, would rise again. I didn't yet have defences against these sentences, but injustice supplied me with the rage necessary to truly exist.

From then on, my revenge would be to excel at everything. I'd stake myself before the world, perfect, until the wrath overflowed. I'd never be a *lettre morte*, a discarded piece of paper. They'd have to notice me.

Go to Sleep, Caroline[28]

LESS THAN A YEAR LATER, MY FATHER GOT A BETTER JOB AT a real estate company, allowing him to rent a seven-and-a-half[29] in Hochelaga-Maisonneuve. Our new apartment was on Sainte-Catherine East, at the corner of Dézéry, directly in front of the stop that Pop's charity truck[30] would make for the neighbourhood junkies and prostitutes, right next to the strip joint. It wasn't a trendy strip club where businessmen in suits might go with their important clients. It was a bar without a sign, a place where Manon, who was missing a few of her front teeth, would dance, or where Natalie would leave her son playing in the aisles while she'd have a quickie with a cop in exchange for a bit of leniency. The place where Gisèle danced. Gisèle, fifty-five years old, five foot three and one hundred and seventy pounds, who'd worked behind the broken glass panel for twenty straight winters, so long that no one noticed her anymore.

It was way before all the gentrification. Before anyone called it HoMa.

HoMa. Oh my god, seriously, give me a fucking break.

For us, it was just our hood, our home, where we lived. Even if our home kept getting robbed. Even if we always had to go inside before night fell, because after 5:00 p.m. the people who lived behind us were way too far gone, and the old man I hated, home from fixing old beaters ready for the scrapyard, was often seized with the urge to beat up his kid. He called him "lil-shit" like it was one word. He'd go, "Git-over-here-you-lil-shit-wait-till-I-git-my-hands-on-you!" We never learned his real first name, so my younger brother and I called him *little pig* because we weren't allowed to swear. That insulted him way more than "little shit." Go figure. But we understood. It was our hood; it was home.

It was home because we knew the names of all the sex workers, the night ones and the morning ones. They knocked on our door sometimes in the winter when something bad happened to them. Something bad other than their miserable lives, I mean. Like having to run away and leave their shoes behind in the middle of winter. We'd lend them what they needed so they could get home since the winds were powerful on Sainte-Catherine Street and there was no Prince Charming on his way to protect them. It wasn't like they had a lot of clothes on to begin with. People often ask me if that's what a little girl remembers: their scanty outfits, their provocative phrases, their fishnet stockings, their occasionally exposed breasts as they got out of cars. No. What I remember most is their hands. The black and pink dirt under their nails, the chipped polish. Their long, skeletal fingers. I never saw any of them wearing gloves, even when it was minus twenty. Except Natalie, when she went to drop her son off at the school bus stop. As soon as she started walking back, she'd take off her coat and her mittens and we'd see her dirty, broken fingernails, her rough, dry hands.

When the song "*Dors Caroline*" came out on video, I shouted, "Hey, that's us!" I didn't get that when they talked about it snowing in Brooklyn, that Brooklyn was in New York. I thought that saying it was snowing in Brooklyn was an expression, like "it's raining cats and dogs." And I thought I heard them say something about the

Jacques-Cartier Bridge.[31] I was pretty proud. Except that in our hood there were no girls who looked like Caroline, with her pink skin, chubby cheeks, and clean hair, as if she'd just left her parents' house in Boucherville, in the burbs. The hookers in our neighbourhood just looked cold all the time.

HoMa, fucking unbelievable, I'll never get over it.

It was home because we knew all the local junkies and we knew how to deal with them, even before we started Grade 4. We knew the last thing you did was call the police: it was better to let them lick their wounds, settle their scores themselves. They never did anything to us if we didn't talk to them, if we didn't provoke them somehow. Anyway, those junkies were all chickenshit. You could read shame and fear in their eyes, which dropped to the ground as if they'd already seen too much.

Hochelag' was just our hood. Nasty, cold, full of dust and concrete. It always reeked too, on Sainte-Catherine East. Hot dogs, dog shit, drunk dude piss, dried semen, old cigarette stubs, cheap beer, the garbage left out on the sidewalk any day of the week, the smell of stale air, even outside. It smelled like junk. It smelled of misery. Unlike in the song, nobody was lost in Hochelag'. Everyone was trapped in poverty, captive of their pasts, their lives hijacked and then imprisoned in solitude.

But over at 3249 Sainte-Catherine East, there lived a family who burst into full-throated belly laughs, who played music to dance to and who, just before evening prayers, told the kids bedtime stories, stories in Spanish with happy endings. I slept like a baby, had warm gloves to confront the chilly winter mornings, good boots to stride confidently into the future. It's true that my mother's hands were dry and rough like those of the girls on the streets, and that her nail polish was peeling. Except her hands smelled like the fake lemon-scented cleaning products she used at her clients' houses, as well as all the food she prepared once she got home: rice, onions, garlic. They smelled like home. They smelled of immigrants, of sacrifice, of communion, of taking the host and believing in Jesus Christ.

The Peanut Butter Solution[32]

OUR PARENTS DIDN'T DO NIGHT SHIFTS ANYMORE, BUT THEY often worked evenings. We still didn't have our papers, and my older brother, who was Cégep[33] age, had to pay the same fees as a foreign student. This was expensive, so he became a busboy. After his classes, instead of studying, he, like my parents, had to clean up other people's filth and crud.

From that point on, my little brother and I were home alone entire evenings, until ten o'clock, which seemed to us like the middle of the night. We slept in my parents' big bed and watched inappropriate programs like *9-1-1* and *Northern Mysteries*, and other trashy stuff that scared us shitless. We huddled together in front of the TV, fear in our bellies, watching other people's catastrophes unfold. I guess it was easier to scare ourselves with the plight of strangers than to confront our own demons, who lived in the back alleys or began walking by our apartment after the sun went down.

As if it wasn't scary enough to be home alone after eight o'clock, I'd turn the TV up to the maximum. Every gunshot shook us, but at least we could focus on the relatively safe feeling of fear for the little African-American criminal getting beaten up by white Baltimore cops rather than our own neighbour shouting, "I'm gonna fuckin' kill him, I tell you I'm gonna KILL him, fuck!"

Each time we found ourselves alone in the dark, we watched shows like these where we were in known territory: instead of imagining the worst, we knew what was coming. Our parents' big bed was our reliable oasis; it barricaded us against the hostility of the world outside, and we could count on it to contain our little trembling bodies. At the back of the bedroom, where the window opened onto the concrete alleyway with its broken bottles and old cigarette stubs, we relied on the TV to exorcise our loneliness and deflect our fears. We could absorb ourselves in improbable dramas taking place far from our home and in another language rather than think about the fact that we'd been left alone, vulnerable, and armed only with a remote control and our small clasped hands. We were always able to fall asleep to *Northern Mysteries* and *9-1-1*.

But the first time, I was frightened. I was the big sister, and I knew I couldn't let my little brother see that I was afraid. My parents had taught me well: don't reveal where fragility meets weakness. I had to take care of him the way women before me took care of their families, and with us Latinas, that meant by providing food. So I cut some celery stalks and filled them with peanut butter. I placed them in a circle on a plate, the way Sister Angèle[34] had shown me on *Télévision Quatre-Saisons*. We ate them as we watched our shows until we succumbed to exhaustion with the TV still on.

Chileans don't eat raw vegetables, especially not like that, as a snack. Nor do they eat peanut butter. When my mother came home after a double shift to find leftover celery sticks filled with peanut butter—a culinary trend not seen since the 1980s—I imagine that she gazed at us with tenderness, sleeping together in her queen-size bed. And as she did, she must have told herself that we were integrating well.

Sky's the limit

WE WERE IN OUR PHYS. ED CLASS AT THE INDOOR POOL AT the Morgan Baths. It was early in the morning, first period, and my eyes were barely open as I was slowly changing into my bathing suit. The schoolyard monitor, who was with us that day, spotted a dark mark in my armpit. The woman immediately informed the teacher, who hurried over to ask me to show her my armpit. Out of surprise, modesty, dignity, or childish obstinacy, whatever it was, I refused. The monitor raised my arm herself to show it to the teacher; she was triumphant when my mark could be seen.

I understood that my refusal would be used against me. I understood that even before I said anything, these women—who felt they were on my side—assumed that we were getting beaten at home. That in their eyes, the spectre of family violence was always a possibility. That physical abuse was part of the equation. Without ever considering that brown skin could just be like that sometimes.

They questioned me while I was naked; then, several other times during the phys. ed class and still again later that afternoon.

They finally let me leave, but I saw a shadow of uncertainty in their gaze. They watched me out of the corner of their eyes for days. I was spied upon and followed around, but I nevertheless behaved nonchalantly, as if I didn't see the question that never left their faces. I spent my days demonstrating that I was happy, playful, and attentive in class, while filling in my Hilroy notebooks: speaking well of my parents so they wouldn't get hassled, telling of family dinners with candles on the table on certain winter evenings, my mother's bubbly laughter, my father's sparkling intelligence. Show that my family was united, but not so much that it sounded suspicious. Clear us of all doubt.

I was always on the alert. I spent my days polishing my act, perfecting my role. I kept it going even when I wasn't being observed. My performance was flawless. By nightfall, I was exhausted.

I scrubbed everything clean, anything that could attract their attention, trying to make sure it wouldn't happen again. Erased whatever was different from what they considered normal. Scoured and polished away whatever failed to jibe with their points of reference. The burden of proof rested on the shoulders of the nine-year-old immigrant in a one-piece yellow bathing suit shivering under the blinking neon lights of the Morgan Baths.

And so I learned to stay in the shadows, allowing only enough light in to reveal the vaguest contours of my life. To present a reflection of a life. To never again fling my arms up to the sky.

Brother André[35]

EVERY DAY, THE EXACT SAME TRIP, THE IDENTICAL ROUTE, no detours. The driver of the yellow École primaire Maisonneuve school bus never went out of his way to be nice to us. He was young, indifferent to the kids he picked up, and fond of driving fast. He had a job, a rare thing for guys his age in our neighbourhood; it gave him a certain dignity, and you could see it, deep in his blue eyes. An actual legal, legit job. It would be pushing it to expect him to be polite or jolly; why would it matter if he had a quick temper?

We kids didn't even know his name. When my friend asked him what it was, he shot back, "What's it to you? Get in my bus, shut your hole, and don't you dare open the window! There's tons of bugs out there." He was a Hochelaga guy, jaded, defensive, suspicious of friendliness. He knew too well it was always safer to remain anonymous.

Every evening we climbed aboard "his" bus. The Haitians, the Vietnamese, and the Latinos greeted him with a courteous *Bonjour, monsieur*.* He answered with a nod, the same one he offered in return for the scarce *Allos*† from the more outgoing Québécois kids. He usually let us make a racket without exercising much discipline, but he did have his days when almost anything could piss him off. On those days we joked that he was having his period that week, unaware that the week invariably coincided with his pay not arriving in time to make his rent on the first of the month. His angry days were easy to see coming. On the days leading up to them, he honked his horn more often, and we could hear him muttering behind the wheel. It just took one kid to open a window and stick his hand outside for him to start railing, threatening to stop the bus on the side of the road and abandon us there. It wasn't exactly a caring kind of discipline, but it was certainly effective. On those cheerless days, we knew we'd better not piss him off by acting like little kids, as he put it; we sat straight and kept our heads down.

We knew it was one of those furious, stormy days when he'd already let out two *Would-you-*SHUT*-up*s? He was clearly finding our rambunctiousness hard on his nerves. Except that day, our driver had taken a different route. I don't know if there was too much snow, or construction, or if he was just as sick of his route as he was with the rest of his life or if, consumed by the thoughts that ate away at him at the end of every month, he'd just taken a wrong turn. In any case, I hadn't recognized my street when he stopped on the south side rather than the north as he usually did; he'd also stopped the bus after the fire station rather than before. I started to worry, and when I looked at my turquoise watch, it was past the time we usually got to my stop. Although I was anxious, I didn't want to bother him, and I naively told myself that he would come back to the exact same place where he was supposed to let me off. Though I knew it was highly improbable.

---

*   Good morning, sir.

†   Heys.

My patience struggled against my growing distress as I watched the other kids get off the bus. Pretty soon no one would be left, and I knew I'd need to pee soon. I almost went to see him, but the farther we got from my stop, the more worried I was that he'd get mad. I didn't even recognize where we were now. I didn't say a word. I stayed hunched down in my uncomfortable seat and stared out the window at the strange surroundings. I prayed that he'd miraculously turn around once he got to the place where he brought the bus back, the place where all the buses went to rest every night. Of course, that would never happen; I knew that. Yet I continued to put off the moment of confrontation.

At the end, I was the only kid left. Our eyes met in the rearview mirror. A frown, a look of shock, quickly followed by frank irritation. "What the fuck are you doing there?"

I answered softly, unaware that my virtuous-little-girl act would only annoy him further. "It's because you didn't really stop at my stop, *monsieur.*"

"What the fuck! Are you fucking kidding me? I stopped on the other side of the street. It's the same fucking thing!"

"But, *monsieur*, I didn't see that from my window."

He expelled all his annoyance and weariness into one long sigh, though not before throwing a murderous glare my way. We drove the rest of the way in silence. I really had to pee now, but I told myself I'd rather die than let him know. He continued to pout and frown for what seemed like an entire winter. He drove impatiently; his exasperation couldn't have been clearer, as if to make me feel guiltier than I already did.

To distract myself from my urge to pee, I argued with him in my head. I'd learned the way by heart, had counted the stops, had learned to spot each of the stores that reassured me we were going the right way. I always sat in the same place, the second to last seat on the left, and I always knew where to get off. I'd followed all the instructions to the letter and no one in the history of my short existence had told me I was supposed to look at both sides of the street.

I liked school and everything that came with it because the world outside was a jungle, while at least the framework of school taught me rules. Sure, some were pretty random or even stupid, but you could easily follow them. Until then, though, I hadn't understood that there were several truths and I always had to be aware of them. Even so, I realized I would never be able to anticipate all of them, no more than I could be confidently sure of my surroundings. I had to keep my eyes open. And be sure not to blink.

The return trip took place in tense silence. My driver drove me to my usual stop, on the right side of the street. Once we'd arrived, I couldn't stay mute any longer. I went down the steps, and just before he closed the squeaky door, I said in a grateful voice: "Thank you, *monsieur*. I'm sorry about the detour."

"It's all right... What's your name?"

"Caroline."

"Carolina?"

"No, Caroline."

"Okay, well, bye, Caro. I'm André, by the way."

"Oh, like Brother André!"

"What? Whose brother?"

"Uh, nothing, it's no one."

I waved to him. He gave me an awkward, forced smile before closing the door, which squealed like a sacrificed pig.

I was chilled to the bone as I ran to my front door and rang the bell. But just before my mother answered it, I peed in my underwear right there on the front steps. When she saw the tear running down my cheek, she attributed it to the shame I must have been feeling about the liquid running down my pants and my purple boots. I didn't tell her anything about my inability to recognize our neighbourhood despite having lived there for two years, or that my driver had never heard of Brother André, whom my mother visited once a month, climbing the steps of Saint Joseph's Oratory on her knees, even if Côte-des-Neiges was on the other side of the world. In any case, she would never have believed me.

The next morning, as I got on the bus, the driver was in a good mood again. The angry clouds had passed.

"Good morning, *monsieur*."

He nodded. "Carolina."

I took a seat in the front of the bus. And I didn't correct him.

Tell me the name of your Cavalier[36]

WE BEGAN GIGGLING THE WAY ONLY A TIGHT GROUP OF little girls can, every time the guy we called "our Cavalier" arrived. Right on time. He'd show up, as regular as clockwork, at exactly five after eight. I'm the one who came up with the name. In Grade 4 I didn't exactly know what a *cavalier* was; I'd just associated the word with someone who suddenly sprang off, the way he did whenever the bell rang. My friends had laughed, and as he was with us most mornings, they'd added "our" to this nickname. He was in his early forties and, like in a bad film, wore a long beige raincoat that came down to his shins, thereby perfectly embodying the cliché of the minor sexual predator, the ridiculous exhibitionist.

For a month, he'd gone unnoticed by the bus drivers, the schoolyard monitors, and all the adults who watched our school-yard. But the four of us had spotted him the first day on account of his nervous tics, his furtive looks, his palpable excitement, and his guilty expression. He used to wait by the fence, next to the prickly bushes and not too far from the school buses parked in single file.

He'd wait until the few parents who were there had deserted the area, leaving the boys to their dodge-ball games and the girls to their tiresome hopscotch, and then he'd get closer to us.

He came slowly, constantly looking from side to side like a hunted animal. But nobody was paying him any attention apart from our gang of chatty little girls, in our pink scarves and patterned barrettes, our French braids under our winter hats and earmuffs already dishevelled before eight-thirty in the morning. He managed to make himself visible only to us and we watched out for him, from a bit closer each time, the way we would for an animal we were trying to tame. He'd wait, anxious, impatient for time to pass, avoiding our eyes until the last few seconds. Within the minute preceding the school bell, that last second when we hardly had the time to see the boys exchange a Wayne Gretzky card for a Mario Lemieux, he'd open his beige raincoat. Wide open.

It had probably been a month that he'd been coming to visit us about two or three times a week. We knew his routine, and he knew ours. After our first encounter, when we'd reacted with shock, we'd gotten used to the idea of another kook in our neighbourhood. He stood in front of the school but a bit in the background, like a tree, immobile, solid, in good weather or bad, and we'd gradually accustomed ourselves to his faithful presence. We'd even gotten to the point where we secretly admired his audacity—October was always pretty cold, even under our hoodies and fleece sweaters. You really had to be nuts to keep up that routine under the pouring autumn rain. As the days got colder, we began to feel a mixture of pity and respect for our faithful horseman.

That morning was no exception. It was the Tuesday after Thanksgiving, and we hadn't seen him for a few days. The leaves had suddenly fallen from the mature trees in one weekend and scattered on the ground; their colours painted the asphalt ochre. Despite the cool temperature, a gorgeous autumn light shone on my friends' faces. Julie had just bitten into her apple—her autumn breakfast, replaced by a banana in the winter—when Mimi screamed, "He's here! Our Cavalier is back!"

"Look, Caroline! He's got a fancy plaid scarf now," said Cathou just before I turned around to get a glimpse of him. It was true, he'd donned a tartan scarf. It was wine-red and forest-green and brought out the lovely green of his frightened eyes. He knew he didn't have much time and he was desperately looking for us. We were hiding behind the main entrance. We had exactly five minutes to let out as much exuberance as possible before the bell, when we'd enter the building in a semblance of silence.

"Should we keep hiding?" said Mimi.

Julie took the time to finish her apple and then casually throw it over the fence before answering. "I dunno. I kinda wanna see."

"We've already seen it, Julie."

"Yeah, but it's really cold. I've never seen one when it gets really cold. Apparently, they shrink!"

The playground monitor turned toward us. There was no way for her to guess what we were laughing about.

"Okay, but we'll wait till the last minute," said Cathou.

We began to watch the monitor's every movement. She was standing with the little first graders, freezing. She was turning the skipping rope with one hand and pulling her turtleneck sweater up over her face with the other. She never wore a coat before the second of November; nobody really understood why, and no one would ask her. In my hood, we didn't ask questions like that. What interested us was the moment she'd smile with relief, right after she glanced at her watch for the tenth time. That would mean that the bell was about to ring and we wouldn't have to wait for our special guest to do his thing. We were on high alert as the rope turned and the little girls chanted, *Crème à la glace, limonade sucrée, dis-moi le nom de ton cavalier.**

We were cold and exasperated. We wiggled our fingers inside our cheap fake wool gloves, rewound our scarves around our faces, hopped in place. A fine rain began to fall, as if the morning drizzle had finally decided to just go for it, drench us in its miserable coldness.

---

*   Ice cream, sweet lemonade, tell me the name of your cavalier.

"Oh no, I'm not gonna see anything," Mimi said, trying her best to wipe the raindrops collecting on the thick lenses of her big glasses.

I was starting to get impatient when Julie elbowed me in the side and said, "This is it. Let's go!" The playground monitor was no longer smiling when I turned toward her, but I trusted Julie. We approached within a few metres of our Cavalier. He was looking around in panic, rubbing his hands together to keep warm, a cigarette between his lips. When he finally stopped rubbing his hands, we knew he'd seen us. He threw his cigarette to the ground without even taking the time to crush it with his heel.

"Okay, girls, get ready," said Julie. "He's gonna take his dick out."

And that is what he did. He opened his beige raincoat just as Julie finished her sentence. I saw his ratty-looking brown wool sweater. Underneath, we could see the top of a white T-shirt. He was wearing lots of layers too, but he wasn't wearing pants, or underwear, just long socks that came almost all the way up to his knees, a bit like the soccer players my dad watched on TV.

He must be cold, I thought.

"It didn't even shrink!" Mimi was right, and we were impressed: his penis was erect, despite the temperature, despite the rain, despite the four little prepubescent girls laughing with their hands over their mouths. The bell sounded. As quickly as he'd opened his raincoat, he pulled it closed, turned on his heels, and ran off before anyone else saw him. It was so fast that I wondered if we hadn't just imagined everything: his penis, his hairy skin, his offence.

This could have gone on for months if it hadn't been for Cathou. She had a crush on a cute boy in our class called Simon. Simon was perfect in all ways, but he could be pushy. He hadn't let up when he spotted Cathou laughing instead of lining up to go inside. She'd explained that it was a secret, but that only had the effect of further piquing his curiosity. He followed her around, nagging her to tell him what was going on until finally, when they were standing at her locker, she gave in. She told him the basic facts about our morning meetings with the Cavalier.

If instead of Simon she'd had a crush on Yannick, the little bad-ass, or on Romeo, who wrestled with his mother's boyfriend, or, in fact, on any other boy, our story would most certainly have remained a funny anecdote the grown-ups never heard about. But Simon came from a different background, practically another planet: his parents were married and still together; he was an only child, loved by his mother and father, who gave him all the attention they could. His mother worked part-time as a nurse; she was involved in the PTA and was always the only volunteer on school outings. She'd come to pick him up in the schoolyard the minute school ended for the day. She was the kind of mother who would ask her son, "How was your day, sweetheart?" as she gave him a piece of fruit for his snack. I don't know what his father's job was, but he would go to work in a white shirt after dropping Simon off at school in the morning. I imagine that his father was the sort of guy who would make conversation at suppertime, ask everyone how their day was. In any case, Perfect Simon evidently failed to keep his trap shut.

I can only imagine his parents' faces, stunned by this piece of news: a sexual predator had been exposing himself to the little girls in an elementary school for weeks without anyone finding out. Of course, the next morning it wasn't our Cavalier who was waiting for us in the schoolyard but the two most dreaded women at our school: the schoolyard monitor and the principal.

They forced us to go through interminable interrogations and made us tell the same story a hundred times, either separately or by turn. It was the principal who was asking the questions, and she had saved me for last.

"What time does the man in the raincoat get here?"

"Just before the bell, *madame*."

"Every day?"

"No, not every day."

"Which days?"

"I don't know. Sometimes he's there and sometimes he's not. We never know in advance."

"And what does he do?"

"Nothing."

"What do you mean, nothing? What did he do the last time?"

"He didn't do anything. He never does anything."

"He never opened his raincoat?"

"Yes."

"That's not nothing."

"Oh, okay."

"So go on. What did he do?"

"Well, he opened his raincoat."

"Okay. And after that?"

"Nothing."

"He didn't show you his penis?"

"No."

"He didn't?"

"Well, no, or, well, yes. But it's because actually, he doesn't show it to us. We saw it because he wasn't wearing underwear. He just stands there with no underwear on."

"And he touches himself?"

"What?"

"Does he touch himself?"

"I don't understand."

"When he shows you his penis, does he touch himself?"

"Uh, no. Well, he can't because he's holding his coat."

I didn't even know what "touching himself" meant. It seemed disgusting. Why was she asking me that? Why would he have done that? During their questioning, the principal had become so serious, I worried I'd done something wrong. I fidgeted in my chair. Maybe I should have claimed he'd touched himself? I was relieved that at least she hadn't asked us why we hadn't told the grown-ups about this. She knew that in our neighbourhood, we didn't call the police or any other authorities, including the schoolyard monitors.

People sometimes ask me when I became political. The thing is, in our neighbourhood, politics knocked at the door and broke windows when we weren't looking. It was there when we lost our neck warmers and it was a big deal for the family budget, when we finally ran into our ghost-neighbours at the supermarket on the first of the month, when we gave our little milk carton to our friend in the morning because her mother had been laid off from one of the factories that was closing, when we passed cops on Sainte-Catherine arresting the big brothers of the girls at the day camp, the brothers who'd become little pimps, but leaving the other ones, the ones who'd become junkies, lying in the street, and every time the government changed and my parents didn't have the right to vote. It wasn't like life was on one side and politics on the other. There were adults and their rules and us, and we tried to find our place, knowing the world to be unjust, power corrupt, and authority sketchy.

"All right. And then, after that?"

"After what, *madame*?"

"After he showed you his penis, what did he do?"

"Nothing. Uh, I mean, he left. He always takes off right when the bell rings."

"And you?"

"Me what?"

"What did you do when he showed you his penis?"

"I laughed."

"YOU LAUGHED?"

"Well, yeah, just a little."

"What was so funny?"

"I don't know. Just his thing."

"His thing? What thing?"

"Under his coat."

"His penis?"

"Yes."

"A man who shows you his penis is funny?"

"I dunno. No?"

"No."

"Okay."

After all those questions, I felt a bit dirty, so I didn't say anything else. I was afraid of being told off and I just felt like crying.

The principal could see that, and she let me go back to class. I don't know if it was out of fear of potential consequences, but our parents were never told. And it was definitely not something we'd be blabbing about at home. But from that day on, the schoolyard monitor never left us alone; she was always spying on us. We knew that each of our movements was scrutinized, each burst of laughter a cause for suspicion. The cops who had begun to park next to the school started to watch us play as well. If the man in the raincoat ever came back, we never saw him.

Our mornings were humdrum once again. To pass the time, we'd gone back to mechanically playing elastics, shouting, "p-i-z-z-a, pizza." A few months later, everyone was talking about École polytechnique[37] and nobody remembered the story about the raincoat anymore. The adults never learned that we'd named the man "our Cavalier" and we never knew his name or whether his penis shrivelled up when the temperature went below zero.

The summer I turned eleven

DESPITE ITS LOCATION AT THE CORNER OF MORGAN AND Adam, a very francophone area, and because it was Protestant, my last elementary school was one of the most multicultural in Montreal. But that clearly wasn't the case at Ratoureux Day Camp, the least expensive camp in the neighbourhood. I didn't know the meaning of the word *ratoureux** but I wasn't thrilled the name contained the word *rat*. We signed up for a few weeks in the summer, along with others from our neighbourhood: kids who arrived late, swearing, wearing the same dirty shorts as the day before, heads full of lice and hearts full of spite. It was noisy, intense, and often violent, but we played outside, and we went swimming a lot, which I especially liked.

I'd made a few friends, not great friends, but girls I could share a joke with. I don't remember their first names or their faces. There were probably some Isabelles, Karines, and Julies again. They

---

* Mischievous, sneaky.

seemed interchangeable and a lot like the other ones around me. Anonymous girls who would not change my life but who kept me company and, in the chaos that constituted day camp, sometimes even held my hand. I almost never spoke to the boys. They were way too rough, especially Tommy. Him, I remember.

Tommy was fat. Not the fat but healthy type, nor fat and jolly, nor even fat but comfortable in his own skin: fat the way poor people can be, fat people who are always hungry. His lunches often consisted of nothing but a Vachon cake[38] and a can of Pepsi. He was aggressive, bad-tempered, and mean. He never spoke, only shouted, threw fits like a two-year-old, like he wasn't nine whole years older than that. He had no father, was neglected by his mother and short-changed by life, but he terrorized all the kids at the camp, especially the smallest ones, every time he had the chance. I didn't mind his harsh personality; I pitied him. Every day I saw his lunches and all his bitterness, and like a super Catholic Latina, thought, "Poor, poor child." I couldn't help but ask myself what kind of mother sent her son to camp looking like he'd spent the night hanging from a clothesline, with a dirty T-shirt on his back, a plastic bag containing a fizzy drink and a Twinkie. At the time I hadn't realized that his mother hadn't sent him to camp with this meal, but with just no lunch at all, and he'd picked this up himself at the depanneur. Poor, poor child.

Halfway through the summer, after three days of uninterrupted rain, the camp was buzzing with energy. The counsellors, who were seventeen or eighteen at the oldest, were running out of ideas on how to channel our boredom-turned-agitation. One smart aleck came up with the great idea of playing flag, which I hated, in the gym, which was too small. Our counsellor named Tommy the captain of the red team. An attempt to use psychology, give Tommy some control over his reality. Another kid who was shy, withdrawn, and unpopular would be the captain of the blues. Taking turns, each child had to put on a blindfold before drawing a scarf of one of the two colours. Then they slipped it in the belt loops of their shorts, kind of like a tail that would connect them to the other members of their team: on one side the blues, on the other the reds.

I went ahead, uninterested in which team I'd end up on; I blindfolded myself and took one of the scarves from the box. Before I could take off my blindfold, I heard Tommy yell. His voice filled the room, bounced off the ceiling before it struck me in the chest. "Oh no, fuck! Not the fat *négresse!*"

He screamed my social status to all in this muggy gymnasium. He was fat too, but he outranked me; I wasn't just round, but a girl who was brown. I was an undesirable.

More than a quarter of a century later, I remember the sharp effect of those words, deep in my flesh. I remember his haircut, the braided rat-tail down his neck. His piercing, menacing blue eyes. How he struggled like a devil in holy water when he felt threatened. His meagre lunches and his cheeks, which were always dirty. The rage in his heart. I remember his first and last name; if he's still alive, he couldn't possibly have any memory of my existence.

A little bully I'd pitied had managed to humiliate me in front of everyone, and even if none of those people meant anything to me, I was dying of shame. I was too mortified to fight back—and a part of me felt that life would probably take care of that anyway.

At lunchtime, he had a detention in a corner of the gym, alone with a counsellor who was trying to convince him to apologize. Meanwhile, I opened my lunchbox. It was a good day. I had an apple, pieces of cheese sliced with love by my mother, grape juice in a little Sun-Maid carton with the white girl in the big red hat, and a tuna sandwich, full of mayonnaise, exactly the way I liked it.

And him: at the age of eleven, his fate was already written in the sky. He'd always be a low-life. He'd grow into a frustrated, miserable delinquent. His fate lay somewhere between drugs, prison, and itinerance. I didn't consider the worst scenario because even at that age I knew that the worst thing that could happen to the kids at camp was way worse than what I could see in the streets of my neighbourhood. His most probable fate: dead before the age of forty. Or dead to the world, at least.

In any case, that day at Ratoureux Day Camp, the red team had their flag stolen pretty quickly. And Tommy and I were united in not giving a fuck.

Swallowed[39]

THE FRENCH LANGUAGE HELD FEW SECRETS FROM ME, AND I was even in the book club at my elementary school. I devoured everything I was given to read. I didn't really choose, since we had a list of suggested titles. We got stars for each book we read, and after we'd read a hundred, we received one as a gift. I'd surpassed the one-hundredth book a long time ago; I'd read almost all the books in the library, my favourite ones more than once.

There was *The Year without Michael*, which had me mesmerized. It told the story of a teenage girl's determined search for her brother, how she uses every means available to her. It seemed he'd run away and had never come home, despite his sister's desperate but futile search for him. I had to borrow it three times in a row; I struggled to understand why someone would want to leave their family. I only had my brothers, my father, and my mother. I knew about my parents' pain at being separated from their families. I knew what it was to grow up without grandparents, aunts, and cousins because of being uprooted. I would never be one of those people who'd slip away and vanish. I could never be *La Femme qui fuit.**

I was going through *The Year without Michael* once more, looking for an answer—how could someone leave their family?—when I noticed *Swallowed.* I still can't explain what the book was doing amid the paltry offerings of the elementary school library, but it was there. And it transfixed me.

The strange title bewitched me. I took it off the shelf. I was immediately absorbed, glued to my chair, unable to put the book down. The sentences never stopped, each followed the next in a way that was impossible to interrupt, I tried to keep up with them and their rhythm by holding my breath, but the commas were the only things I could grasp to catch some air. It was the first time a book had been able to suppress the thoughts in my head. I was riveted, held captive by this book. I didn't notice the time; when our library period was over, I had to hurry to check it out.

To this day, I still don't understand why the librarian didn't say anything when I borrowed it, why she didn't frown to see the eleven-year-old Latina leave with Réjean Ducharme. She normally had things to say about the books I chose. "Oh, you're going to like this one, Caroline!" or "Really? Are you sure? I think you're going to find this book a bit boring. You don't want to get this one instead?" This time she said nothing, and her body language certainly betrayed no reaction, no astonishment. Nothing that might have me suspect the incongruity of holding it in my little brown hands. Up until I attended Cégep, I actually thought *Swallowed* was a children's book.

Sometimes I wonder if she was the one who placed it next to *The Year without Michael,* to shake me up, or at the least, to broaden my horizons. If I was ready to relentlessly reread that story about a sudden disappearance that is never resolved, that ultimate abandonment, perhaps, thought she, I was ready to take on Ducharme.

---

*   A novel by Anaïs Barbeau-Lavalette (Márchand de feuilles, 2015). The title means "the woman who flees." The book was translated into English as *Suzanne* (Coach House Books, 2017).

She was Haitian. I like to imagine that she saw in my taste in books an obsession with decimated families, great solitudes, people who slip away from us, wounds that scar us. She often asked me questions about my country of origin. I always felt I successfully evaded them, but I am sure she wasn't fooled. Every dodge told her I had demons I was trying my best to stifle. Opening my eyes to literature may have been her way of telling me that it was, in fact, possible to escape.

From the first few lines, I was left reeling. It just devastated me.

The book transformed my relationship with the French language and, consequently, with literature. It was the first time that I'd found a form of play embedded in words, and that I perceived the beauty of a complex piece of writing without necessarily grasping its entire meaning. Poetry took on a meaning quite different from the very vertical acrostics we saw in class. It was then that I learned that it is possible to be wounded by those we love, that love is partly comprised of loneliness, and that childhood is not the age of innocence. I understood who I was. I saw that excess was salvation; absoluteness became enchanting, upheaval essential. Through words, I could perhaps recover a bit of the little Caroline whose fire had diminished over the years. Violence now seemed ordinary, and sorrow was no longer opposed to light.

I would not return to Chile before I became an adult because I didn't want to have to grieve more loss. I hated departures and I spent many years struggling with the social and cultural distance that was growing between me and my parents. I understood that French was becoming my language, slowly superimposing itself onto Spanish despite this latter being my first language, my mother tongue. And French would become a place in which I would reside. It would be this language that would not only allow me to say what I needed to, and to understand the world, but also to grow distant from my own people. Grow distant from them without leaving them.

Swallowed made me who I am. The day I discovered Ducharme, the French language gave me a voice. And one day I'd use it to tell my own story.

Shit, Lola

THE WELCOME CLASS WAS IN THE DISTANT PAST. IT HAD been five years since I'd left it for the regular stream. I was in Grade 6 at the same school, and I finally had some good friends. In the schoolyard, when we played barbecue tag and the boys ran after the girls to extract kisses, I got chased too. Not by the ones I liked the most, but still, I no longer had to wait around in humiliation hoping to be chosen or, even worse, pretend to be chased like the two or three reject girls did. When recess time came, they pretended to be busy with some sort of game plan, but they fooled no one. Girls didn't choose their suitors and it would never have occurred to me to question this state of affairs. Instead, I passively waited to be selected.

My best friends and I judged girls who French-kissed with a mixture of curiosity, envy, and incredulity. We'd already learned the codes imposed on girls: you had to be experienced but not slutty, sassy but not bitchy, seductive but not a tease, and you had to glide across this tightrope as if you'd been born knowing how.

This tightrope was so thin it was impossible to keep your balance as you made your way across, yet we kept getting on it every day; it had come to replace hopscotch. Maybe more than the other girls, *les québécoises*, I felt the need to juggle these conventions and perform this fantastical idealization of feminine identity. When a boy caught me, I let out a little shriek, pretended to be surprised, and giggled as I allowed a kiss on the cheek. Kisses on the mouth were reserved for my crushes, who were numerous and ever-changing, and who had already rested their lips on my cheeks. The few times this happened, it constituted an event that earned an entry in my diary and a bit of gossip with my friends.

I remember feeling I had arrived, that I was finally part of the gang. I had my own place in our eclectic group of chatty friends, which itself had its own place in the schoolyard, not too low on the social ladder, at a comfortable distance from the vertiginous top. I was doing very well in all subjects at school, especially French and English. Those hard times were over, I felt. There were a few racist jerks at École secondaire Chomedey, which was right next to our elementary school, and they would occasionally come over and throw snow-covered eggs at us. But otherwise, everything was okay. I finally fit in.

At night I applied myself to my homework and to studying the way only a daughter of refugees can, as if the future of the South American continent depended on it. If I couldn't solve a math problem, I sometimes spent hours sweating over it, not leaving my room even to eat, only emerging once I'd figured it out. My idea of fun was French spelling and grammar. I'd learned all the rules and memorized most of the exceptions; my perfect marks on dictations and all the books I'd read proved my progressive assimilation of this language. Fortunately, afterwards, I let myself collapse in front of the TV for a well-deserved bit of relaxation: to watch my favourite show: *Chambres en ville.*[40]

I enjoyed knowing that my friends were watching the same show at their houses. And what a show! I admired the independence of the Cégep students who boarded at Louise's house. Their families lived far away. I felt I'd never be able to leave home and live in an apartment at that age, not with Latino parents. The girls living there were totally free, and even the plainest among them ended up kissing one of the guys, like Olivier, Pete, or the cute one, Gabriel. My secret idol was always Lola. She was ferocious, strong, wild, even fierce. She would never have pretended to be surprised by a kiss on the cheek, nope, not her.

I wanted to be like her, like all of them. They studied, but they spent the better part of their time drifting from one romantic relationship to another. They lived together in a community, with all the constraints that come along with that, all the heartbreaks and betrayals. But most importantly, they belonged.

I was in my last year of elementary school and already dreaded starting high school. I'd have to change schools again, prove that I had a place there. I told myself I could become like them later. I certainly wasn't afraid of drama, and I was ready to have my heart go through the wringer if it meant I could finally belong to a group where I had a defined role and identity. I wanted to be with them, belong to their universe. Seeing them every evening was a source of oxygen for me; I held my breath or gasped or gulped down air, in accordance with their whims and emotions. I inhaled giant breaths of clichés.

The next day if there was no barbecue tag happening at recess, our group of friends would talk about the episode from the night before. "She's out of her mind," one of us would say, referring to the way Lola was dressed. "She's such a prude," we all said about Annick. "She looks like a bimbo," we said of Vanessa. We learned to scrutinize our sisters according to society's expectations of us, internalizing the codes that restricted and limited who we ourselves could be. I was growing to be an expert in all of this, learning all the social conventions, the forbidden behaviours, the occasions that permission was granted, the fortuitous passes, the attenuating circumstances. I rehearsed the rules, made them my own, and appointed myself the judge. Along with my friends, I triumphed at this challenge: at twelve, our assimilation of these gender codes was in all respects impeccable.

One day, a day like any other, I whirled around with my friends in the schoolyard, gossiping about the latest episode of *Chambres en ville*. I was feeling sure of myself, and carefree.

"Did you see Lola's face yesterday?" asked my best friend.

"When those guys who were cruising tried to pick her up? Yeah, I know, she was really pissed off! It was too funny!"

"What did you say? *Cru—eez—ing*? That sounds so gross! It's *cruising*, not *cru-i-sing*. Ha ha! Hey, you guys, did you hear what Caroline said? Miss Top Student actually got something wrong!"

And yet I practised my new words and expressions aloud every evening. But that word hadn't stuck, and I couldn't find it in the dictionary. I'd repeated it, enunciating every sound the way we did in Spanish. What an idiot. Of course, it was pronounced *cruising*. I'd learned all the rules, but I got it wrong.

I was mortified. It was so humiliating; French was supposed to be my strength. After my friends laughed at me that day, I clammed up. I didn't say another word all day. Pete and Lola became strangers to me that night. How could I have thought I could possibly be in their realm? I knew very well that neither he nor she would have been my friends in real life. We weren't a gang; they talked to each other, and I watched them doing their thing, the way I did with my friends, my classmates, the whole universe.

I suddenly thought of Julien, personified by Gregory Charles,[41] who, starting with the first episode, had to both confront racism at the rooming house and carry a knife at Cégep to protect himself from other Black people. He wasn't safe anywhere.

I changed the channel. From that day on, I only watched American TV shows.

Package deal

WHEN I BEGAN HIGH SCHOOL, MY PARENTS HAD SUCCEEDED in saving up enough money to get away from it all—the drudgery of their working lives—and pay for a vacation in Cuba.

They were proud to tell us the news; after years of hard labour, they had reached this rung on the social ladder. But they warned us: we wouldn't be like other tourists. We wouldn't be like those passing strangers who dream only of taking advantage of what the island offered—beaches and idleness, privileges inaccessible to Cubans— and then simply return to their better lives elsewhere. No, we would be exemplary; we would never cease to express the fraternity that linked us to the people living there. We were basically like Cubans: leftist Spanish speakers from Latin America, raised from birth with revolutionary ideals and constrained to live in a capitalist world.

We talked to all the chambermaids, not because we were nice, nor out of politeness or charity, but out of true friendship. My mother had the exact same job in Canada. Every worker was a comrade, and I learned the whole history of Cuba at Playa Girón in the Bay of Pigs. I'd been hearing my father's socialist monologues my whole life, but here the subject of politics emerged in conversations with ordinary people on the street. Unlike in Montreal, nobody asked us where we were from here; we had black hair and brown skin, spoke Spanish, and laughed heartily. But when we said we were Chilean, big warm and welcoming smiles broke out on these faces that resembled ours.

Then they'd start talking to us about President-Comrade Salvador Allende, about the coup d'état, Pinochet's horrific crimes, and about the involvement of the United States. They spoke of the friendship of our peoples, and of the luminous words of Pablo Neruda. And together, before every meal, we sang the moving song "*Hasta Siempre.*" I closed my eyes, absorbing the hypnotic lyrics. At night—after the torrential daily rains that never lasted more than a few minutes—I repeated the words to myself before falling asleep. *Aquí se queda la clara/La entrañable transparencia/De tu querida presencia/Comandante Che Guevara.** I trembled to the rhythm of their guitars, of their singing and of their struggles.

For the first time, I felt positive about my identity. I was no longer *the one who isn't from here*, just some immigrant. I had become a proud Latin American.

We relished every day by the sea; we had suffered its absence for such long years, whereas it had once been both the beacon and horizon of our existence. We made a point of going only to beaches that were open to Cubans, never those reserved for tourists. From the very first day, my mother became friends with a woman who ended up spending hours at the beach with us. The two of them chatted as if they'd known each other for years while we built our sand empires or ran to catch the waves, which always got away.

This Cuban woman liked me in particular; she called me *mi muñeca*, my doll. A few days before we left, she gave me a queen conch shell. It was giant and all pink inside. She said it was so I'd

---

* Here stays the clear/And fond transparency/Of your dear existence/ Comandante Che Guevara.

always be able to hear the Caribbean Ocean, with its incessant but irregular rhythm. At the time I thought I would keep it my whole life, knowing what it represented for a Cuban living in privation to find a gift to offer someone from another country. But even more importantly because it would remind me of these times we met, when I began to see a new way of existing in the world, one involving a collective identity tied to these Latin Americans who had welcomed me with open arms.

The day of our departure, our parents had to pack. We didn't want to stay with them while they did that, busy as we were filling our lungs with sea air. The Cuban woman kindly offered to stay with us. While my little brother dug in the sand, she began asking me questions about the differences between Chile and Canada. My memories of my mother country were dusty and unclear. I couldn't tell her much about Chile. I took a long time to answer, remaining vague, imprecise, at best hesitant, and I noticed her boredom and irritation deepen on her tanned face.

After a few of my fruitless attempts at explanations, so vague they confused her, she sighed in exasperation. She tried one more question: she asked what I missed the most about Chile. After thinking for a moment, I said, "*Nada,*" nothing. I perceived the irritation in her voice as she said, "Well, anyway, you're not a real Chilean. In fact, you aren't even a real Latina."

I was completely shaken. I answered that since I had arrived at Playa Girón, I seemed to have heard that everyone thought I was Cuban.

She laughed, not in a mean way, but maybe with a touch of condescension. "I knew you weren't a real Cuban the first time I saw you. It's obvious from metres away."

I was skeptical. I saw myself every day in the mirror: my high cheekbones, my plump lips, my dark brown eyes, my hair so black it looked blue, the colour of my skin. "How could you have guessed that? I am Latina. I'm like all the other Latinas."

She smiled sadly, this time with a certain tenderness. "*No, mi muñeca,* you, you are fat, while everyone here is starving to death."

PART III

Where the mothers planted their silence,
their angry daughters sit to uproot it.
—*Ijeoma Umebinyuo*

La grande noirceur[42]

IN CHILE, ON AN OLD DIRT ROAD SO WINDING YOU CAN BARELY call it a road, just a track left by all the footsteps that have come along, a thirty-two-year-old man notices the most beautiful girl he's seen in years. Delicate, with pale eyes, a round, moon-shaped face like a Russian girl's, she walks with a willful stride, holding her recalcitrant little brother's hand. It's not like a movie; their eyes don't meet, but he does see her. He sees her so well that when she disappears behind a door to go inside her house, he cannot stand losing sight of her. He tells himself that she's the one, that it will be her, the right one, if only he dares to act. He has to have her.

He knocks on the door that swallowed up the young beauty to meet her parents and, following the custom, asks her father for her hand. The father immediately accepts. How could he refuse? After a work accident, in addition to being poor, he has become blind and knows he cannot offer his daughter a decent life. The suitor standing before him now is a serious man. A tall man. He has the respectable trade of sailor and is white. The father consents to the marriage right then and there. The girl has no say in the matter. She is only sixteen.

From what we would now call a conjugal rape, but which was then known as a Catholic marriage, my mother was born.

To be honest, I'm not sure my great-grandfather was the one who was blind. That might have been his son—my grandmother's brother. I don't know where the objective truth lies here; it doesn't change anything in our family history. What is certain is that they were poor, lacking the basic necessities of life, ensnared in that extreme kind of misery that eats away at people, destroys their health, crushes their bodies. The work they did was gruelling, and the wages they earned only managed to attenuate, never satisfy, their hunger. This leaves physical traces: it leaves people exhausted, worn out. The misery of impoverished workers marks their bodies, causes faces to sag and backs to curve. It destroys knees, etches wrinkles around the eyes; it degrades, ages, and damages. So I don't know for sure that my grandfather was blind, but blindness would have been an unremarkable thing to happen to someone like him. It was that level of misery, the great darkness.

Most Latin American families are engulfed by secrets they hardly know how to keep. Even over eight thousand kilometres from our country of birth, our family was no exception. My maternal grandfather, the thirty-two-year-old man, was not my biological grandfather. I know only the vague contours of this story from a confession my mother made to me on the phone, in a fit of tears. "*¡Nunca tuve padre! ¡El hombre que tu llamas tu abuelo me dio solo su nombre!*" *

She hurled this at me in the dramatic tone of *telenovelas*,† which was the norm at our house.

When I was little, I often wondered how my grandmother could be at once so devout and tortured by sin. I didn't know what

---

* "I've never had a father! The man you call your grandfather gave me nothing but his name!"

† Soap operas.

consumed her so. Years later, I learned that she'd fallen in love with a different man from the one who was sixteen years older than her and to whom she'd been married without her consent.

She'd had a liaison with this other man, who was married and never committed to her. While her life may have been a suffocating prison, she'd dug herself a trench, allowed herself a margin of freedom. However, it later drove her mad, due to the Christian guilt that kept her on her knees. She would remain a recluse her whole life. She was stuck in a hole, and the more she tried to claw her way out, the deeper it got. Stricken with disgrace and ravaged by shame, she would never forgive herself this lapse.

From what was then called the devil's temptation, but what we would now call a great, doomed love story, my mother was born.

The Shimmering Beast[43]

I'VE ALWAYS LOVED TO SNOOP THROUGH PEOPLE'S DRAWERS. I
used to think it started with immigration and the search for my
shimmering beast—a search for the enigmatic identity stashed in
the bottom of a dresser, stored with the hope of never thinking
about it again, as if the past could be buried in furniture. How not
to lose sight of my intrinsic self when, for the sake of acceptance, I
learned the codes, sang them together with the others; their life as
a chorus, mine in lip-synch? How to fit into their picture, even if
it was dull and meant draining some colours from my days? How
could I avoid stifling myself, losing the person I had been, and still
have a feeling of belonging?

Yet my mother has assured me it's not about that at all. She
says I've been that way for as long as she can remember, that
despite many warnings, I always persisted in crossing boundaries
and invading the personal lives of others. When I was barely three
apples tall, she said, I'd accompanied her to her friends' houses for

tea, and if she lost track of me for thirty seconds, I'd take off to investigate her friends' private lives.

She loves reminding me of the most embarrassing incident, the one in Chile, at her best friend's house. Soon after we arrived, following the customary greetings, I quickly found the master bedroom door, which was closed. Once I'd snuck inside, my domestic archaeology project had no limits. I explored the drawers of the night tables, which were at the perfect height for a three- or four-year-old snoop—and I proceeded to empty them. Diary and dildo in one hand, I continued to scrape away at the bottom of the drawer.

As soon as the women's conversation began to wane and they began clearing away the cups, I knew that the countdown was on. While I was trying to put the diary back in its exact place, the vibrator slipped out of my hands. Attempting to pick it up, I tipped the contents of the drawer onto the floor: anti-aging creams, lubricant, a cream for vaginitis, massage oil, a rosary, cards with prayers to the Virgin Mary, used Kleenex. My mother, upon seeing this jolly mess, burst out laughing. Then, in confusion, she apologized and cut her visit short, saying I was a wayward, foolish child. As usual, the trip home was full of her rebukes, but these never had much of an effect on my shenanigans.

Once we'd settled in Québec, I snooped through my parents' drawers a countless number of times; their bedroom was the locus of my explorations. I went into their closets, made an inventory of each slip of paper I found in their dressers, went through the shoeboxes my parents used as their safes. I often thought I was on the threshold of a revelation as I dissected the contents of some badly sealed envelope. Each time, however, I was overcome with disappointment: faded postcards, tearful letters from my grand- mother and my aunts—women who remained custodians of emo- tional bonds even when a whole continent separated them, their prayers ceaselessly repeated—old photographs of places where we'd lived, already scrutinized a hundred times. I never found any secrets there. My parents' drawers were nostalgia turned museum.

In one of the drawers, the one on the top right, my mother kept her memories of us: old school certificates, badly drawn birthday cards, arts and crafts projects, Mother's Day messages, elementary school report cards, souvenirs of our accomplishments, junk whose sole purpose was to conserve the memory of our childhoods, which had slipped through her worn labourer's fingers because she was so often away. The thought made her suffer and she expressed it from time to time: "*Me perdí los mejores años.*" *

She had indeed sacrificed everything for us, including the possibility of being with us. It was her absence that spoke of her devotion. Needless to say, she visited this drawer regularly, searching for the light of our childhood, endlessly wondering if this eclipse had been worth it.

---

* "I missed your best years."

The woman who planted trees[44]

YOU HAVE TO HAVE SPENT TIME WITH THE ILLITERATE TO recognize the terror concealed in their eyes. The fear of being found out. These people come up with ways to hide their condition, learning methods to dupe the unsuspecting by heart. But their carapaces are made of fear and palpitations, and they tremble. It takes just one false move in their usual choreography for their fingers to shake, for their confidence to shatter.

Thanks to my mother, I often witnessed this ballet of shadow and doubt. She was the best at detecting this alarm hidden deep in their eyes. She invited them to our house. I remember the first one the most.

Every week, following the interminable Dominican Mass, my mother brought home a parishioner. Brimming with Christian goodwill, she took it upon herself to teach a Guatemalan refugee to read. He used my old school notebooks from Chile. They were filled with little drawings; I had used them myself to learn to read and write in Spanish.

He'd sit in the chair that was the farthest from the window, in half-light. He was a man who'd learned to be careful in all his movements; he had sharp reflexes. He'd relied on his memory to learn everything he knew. He hid in the shadows, his entire life a twilight existence. I'd go sit next to him, pretending to do my homework, but I couldn't stop myself from observing him. At the age of ten I could already see the humiliation under his skin.

Mi.

Mamá.

Mi mamá.

*Mi mamá me ama.**

He'd look at simple, childish sentences and be unable to decipher them. And even if he succeeded one day, I wondered, what use would it be to him to read these inanities? *Mi mamá me ama.* In what situation could this not-so-young, childless bachelor, alone in a country that was not his own, silently washing dishes in a seedy east-end resto-bar, make use of the phrase *Mi mamá me ama?* He sat perfectly still, a glazed expression in his eyes, one elbow resting on the table.

Until that Sunday afternoon in February of 1990. It was a sunny day, a day of incandescent beauty. One of those winter days when the air is cold, the ground shimmering. It had snowed earlier, and the city had come to a stop. My mother, always elegant for Mass, looked radiant, and the frost on the windowpanes sparkled. Sitting at the little kitchen table with the slightly sticky transparent plastic tablecloth, I beheld a moment of rare luminosity: one where an adult reads words he understands for the first time.

Mamá

Mi mamá.

---

* My.

Mom.

My mom.

My mom loves me.

I witnessed it there, on my uncomfortable little chair, a pencil in my mouth. I saw him read the words aloud, underlining them with his finger as he went along. Taking his time, he pronounced the sounds correctly in his hoarse voice: *Mi mamá. Mi mamá.* He closed his eyes a few seconds. He repeated: *Mi mamá. Mi mamá. Mi mamá.* He opened them again, and the sharp wariness had left his eyes and made room for something mild and sweet, something like a new clarity. A huge weight had flown off his shoulders, which he now straightened. A tear came to wash away his fear. While the light in his eyes grew warmer, I understood that I had been a fool. *Mi mamá* were the two most beautiful words in the world.

They worked for weeks. Little by little, he learned to decipher all the syllables. He read slowly, painfully, but he was reading complete sentences. This man without any family had just crossed to the other side. He would never be alone again. The thread had been resewn. From now on he was connected to the other humans, those from before, those far away. It was *mi mamá* who had given him a filiation, right in the middle of his first winter.

This moment of splendour turned out to be brief. I still had a knot in my stomach. All this work, these interminable hours. He was thirty-eight years old and had just begun to read in Spanish. He still had to learn French, and my mother couldn't help him with that. There would be a long road ahead before his eyes could completely lose their gloom.

Cité Rock Détente[45]

SHE ALWAYS LISTENED TO THE RADIO WHILE DOING THE interminable chores that came with having a family with three kids. But instead of listening to the raucous private stations, my mother listened to 107.3 FM, Cité Rock Détente, the station domestic workers and housewives turned to for support as they did the kind of work that soils your hands and wears out your soul.

It would never have occurred to them to listen to Radio-Canada. The state radio tried to speak to its citizens; my mother, however, was not a citizen and never related to any of the topics they dealt with. Sure, they sometimes discussed immigration, but as if it was a complex question that required explanations by specialists. They talked about *them*, the immigrants, as if they couldn't hear, the way you talk about someone who is not in the same room. The experts could describe different facets of the immigration issue at length without ever thinking of offering the microphone to immigrants themselves. Apart from *La Rumba du Samedi** on CISM, my mother much preferred her radio to talk about universal themes: love, loss, sorrow, and loneliness. That's what affected her; in fact, it consumed her.

So she bleached the bathroom to Bruno Pelletier,[46] "*Le Temps des cathédrales*," † changed dirty sheets to Julie Masse,[47] "*C'est zéro*," ‡ did the dishes to Marie-Denise Pelletier,[48] "*Tous les cris les S.O.S.*," § and, if she was lucky, left for her night shift on an old tune from the sixties, her all-time favourite, "*Tous les garçons et les filles.*" ¶ Nice, clean, sad songs to accompany her domestic melancholy.

I listened to those songs with her so often that they filled my head. It is to Cité Rock Détente, more than to fairy tales or Disney movies, that I owe the heteronormative romanticism that guided my life as a young girl for so long. More to the point, I learned French alongside my mother with Roch Voisine,[49] Ginette Reno,[50] Marjo,[51] and Gerry Boulet[52] as our teachers. We both learned the innumerable words to say *love*, *weariness*, and *abandonment* in Québécois slang. Thus, you could say we slipped into this new culture through the back door. Through music that comes on at closing time (Marie Carmen,[53] "*L'aigle noir*" **), music that helps kill time when you're in the waiting room at social services (Éric Lapointe[54], "*N'importe quoi*" ††), the kind that plays to foil the monotony of lining up at the bank to deposit the measly cheques paid under the table for washing windows (Luc de Larochellière,[55] "*Sauvez mon âme*" ‡‡). Music that felt and conveyed my mother's exhaustion and heartache.

---

* Saturday Rumba.
† The time of cathedrals.
‡ It's zero.
§ All the cries, the SOS's.
¶ All the boys and girls.
** The black eagle.
†† Meaningless; unimportant.
‡‡ Save my soul.

I often heard various dime-store intellectuals refer to Cité Rock Détente condescendingly as "Cité Rock Matante."* But it was my teacher and my mother's only real Québécoise friend for years.

Cité Rock Immigrantes.

---

* Mom Radio

It's a quarter to twelve and the cleaning lady's in the hallway dispelling mirages[56]

ONE OF FEMINISM'S EARLY TRIUMPHS WAS TO LIBERATE white women from some of their domestic tasks, which were transferred to immigrant women like my mother, who were now both housekeepers at home and servants in the homes of fancier folks. Until her retirement, my mother cleaned the bathrooms of those who had more important or less disgusting things to do.

As these perfectly respectable people always paid her under the table, she had neither sick days nor vacation, and when her employers left on a trip, she found herself on forced unpaid leave. Best-case scenario, she'd get a Christmas bonus if the mistress of the house was feeling charitable, but she could never count on that. The husbands didn't get involved at all; it was their wives' job to hire, order around, and fire my mother. The husbands had more noble things to do. They pulled money out of their wallets, but otherwise we never saw them.

We called them rich people's houses, even if it was just people richer than us, which wasn't hard to be, at least not in the beginning.

As soon as we went inside, my mother began her routine: first the kitchen, then the bathroom, finishing with the bedrooms and the living room, and, if there was one, the office. In fact, there always was one, even if it wasn't used most of the time. She didn't have a minute to waste and neither did I. It wouldn't be long before I wandered off. She had a choice: spend her precious time watching me and telling me off or letting me do what I wanted.

"*Deja todo exactamente donde lo encontraste por lo menos.*" *

"Of course, *Mamita.*"†

I have no idea how many drawers I opened during those years when I followed my mother to dozens of rich people's houses. Underwear drawers, night-table drawers, entire chests of drawers, even drawers under beds. Doors too—kitchen cabinets, fridges, everything from little cupboards to walk-in closets.

I didn't just walk around the rooms opening doors and drawers; I absorbed the lives displayed before me as if I were living them. I analyzed every detail. The books, the paintings, the bottles of liquor, the family photos, the knick-knacks. I took in all the cultural, social, artistic, and even culinary information from these people I didn't know.

I snooped around and analyzed these people's lives. Meanwhile, they had no idea how we lived; often, they had no awareness that I existed at all. My mother and I knew everything about them: their eating habits, the personal care products they used, and the ones they left around for show. We knew when they slept in separate bedrooms, when they had mice, when the women had their periods or no longer had them, when the daughters of good families took secret pregnancy tests, and when the sons in private schools took drugs. We knew who believed in God or in homeopathy, who believed that women came from Venus or who needed chicken soup for the soul. We knew who was on antacid tablets, or antidepressants, or tranquilizers, or sleeping pills. We knew who had marital, school, or financial problems, who struggled with alcohol

---

* "At least leave everything exactly where it was."

† Mommy.

or with an eating disorder. We knew who was dirty, or lazy, or snobbish, or all of those at the same time.

Beneath the clean surfaces that my mother uncovered was their filth. Their little hairs in the shower, their traces of shit in the toilet, and of pee next to it, their spots of spit on the bathroom mirror, their fingerprints on all the tables, their blood and their semen on the sheets. My mother was the magician who made all of that disappear while straining her back, wrecking her hands, and inhaling chemical products that would one day make her sick.

I would have spat in their faces, these women who always smiled as they said nice things about my mother, using the possessive pronoun *my*. "My cleaning woman is a gem," as if she belonged to them, as if they were talking about a dress they'd found on sale, and which looked marvellous on them. Some of them even had the audacity to carelessly add, "Natalia is part of our family," while my mother emptied the vacuum cleaner of their hair, fingernail clippings, crumbs fallen from their mouths, and all their other garbage.

Sometimes they would leave passive-aggressive notes on the sideboard by the front door: "Natalia, don't forget to clean the mirror in the guest bathroom, we're having important guests this evening. Have a wonderful, sunny day!" Or worse, they'd ask for extra chores to be done, without offering to pay a penny more: "Natalia, could you please wash the cutlery, just this once, please? We are having company tomorrow night. Thank you, you are a godsend!"

Immigrant women paid under the table never say no. My mother said, "Yes, of course," and fumed in silence, and I learned to feel contempt. At suppertime, despite her protests, I called her clients "that old bag, that filthy lady, that disgusting family, those dirty snobs in their stinky house." And when my no-paid-sick-leave mother said, "I'm sorry, I can't clean your house anymore—I have too many clients right now and they all live in the same area, near me," it was a lie. For months she'd been counting how many more times she'd need to come to finish paying for her car, her washing machine, or the laptop she'd bought on credit, before she could drop the difficult client, the snob, the racist with zero self-awareness.

From the first of the little notes left here and there and the *Yes, sure*s that had followed, the counting had begun. My mother was too polite and grateful to be working to call her clients shitty people, but her daughter, who spoke without an accent, never held back.

When her clients' children became teenagers, it got even worse. They had parties the moment their parents left the house. They were so used to Natalia and her legendary docility that they never even considered she might betray them; she would never say a word. And she understood that in these circumstances, they were the bosses.

One day, a thirteen-year-old boy whose parents had gone away asked my mother to clean the stove. He'd warmed up some frozen spaghetti his mother had left him for lunch. He'd forgotten to turn off the stove and it had boiled over, burned the saucepan, and splattered everywhere. I watched my mother scrub the stovetop, the surrounding walls, and the floor for an extra hour while he sat in his boxers watching TV, eating a pizza he'd ordered to replace the spaghetti. She washed his plate after he finished eating while he called out, without turning from the TV screen, "Ah, thanks, Natalia. You're the best."

Whenever I become completely livid just because someone speaks too familiarly to my mother, calling her by her first name rather than *madame*, addressing her with *tu** instead of *vous*,† I can feel it all coming back. That's where the anger stems from. The image of my mother on her knees, her head lowered as she cleans the bathrooms, receiving orders, even politely expressed ones, from a child; I will always be on the side of the humiliated. That's where I've burrowed and remain entrenched.

---

*   The informal you.

†   The formal you.

Burst my bubble

IT COULD NEVER BE SIMPLE—HAD TO BE TORTUOUS AND complicated. For as long as I can remember, the women in my family have made up unbelievable stories to camouflage truths that are actually inoffensive and warn us of some great danger. My mother was the master of these implausible and apocalyptical stories. Like her own mother before her, she made one up every time she was worried about us. It was only natural for a Catholic Latina expatriate to make worry part of her identity—a tattoo, a way of life. Not only had she fled a country where people used to disappear, but no matter where she went in the world, her God was punitive. She feared the unknown. Apprehension was the air she breathed.

Our world was wrapped in precariousness and uncertainty over which she had no bearing. She assuaged her need for control on trifles, small things that might affect our bodies. To dissuade me from swallowing my bubble gum, she always told me the same story with the same words, the same intonations, the same ending. She could have simply said, "That couldn't be very good for your health" or

"It might give you a stomachache." She didn't even have to explain anything; she could have just told me not to do it, but I was stubborn, and she had a sense of drama.

She would tell me over and over that when she was little, she'd swallowed a piece of chewing gum that ended up getting stuck to her stomach and causing horrible cramps. She was sent to Emergency for surgery. They opened her stomach and tried to dislodge that damn, tenacious wad of gum. After considerable difficulty, the doctors finally succeeded, and the stitches they used to sew her back up formed a picture of the Big Bad Wolf from Little Red Riding Hood. At this point in the story, she'd lift up her sweater to show me a scar, proof of her sufferings: a long, horizontal line crossed her lower stomach where the lancet had glided over her delicate skin. I felt the cold blade that had pierced her skin all the way down my back and I spat out my gum (on the sidewalk rather than in a garbage can, as a protest), never suspecting that this scar was due to the successive Caesareans caused by three difficult births.

I wasn't traumatized by this horror story, however; way worse ones haunted our family lore. After all, I came from South America, where everyone thinks their family was struck by a wicked spell, that life is a tragedy because God and the vengeful spirits are constantly punishing the innumerable sins, real or suspected, of our ancestors or other, far worse ones we will commit someday. I confess the very abundance of stories lessened their impact. For every prohibition we were supposed to swallow, there was an equally terrible and upsetting anecdote.

When I was a teenager, my mother ordered me to dry my hair before going outside in the winter. She knew someone who'd told her that a woman in her family had caught pneumonia when her long, curly hair had frozen outside. "*Nosotras no somos hechas para el invierno mijita,*"* she'd repeat each time, as if that was actually a logical conclusion. The girl's mother was Madame Sepúlveda, whom she'd met at the Latin American church. She'd had to stay

---

* "We weren't built for winter, my little one."

in hospital, and when she was released, she'd had to stay in bed for weeks. I knew her; she was the cousin of a little girl who was in the group of altar servers, Los amigos de Jesús,* and I never missed the chance to remind my mother that the young woman was also a smoker who ate nothing, drank a lot, hung out with cokeheads she'd been meeting in discotheques since her *quinceañera*† and that the source of her pneumonia might be revealed in her lifestyle habits of prancing around on Saint-Laurent in high heels without a coat on, rather than her wet perm in February. I also reminded her that the old lady, who had one son in prison and another in the United States, wound up falling gravely ill and dying of sorrow, and that she should probably abstain from worrying about such nonsense if she wanted to avoid the same fate. Then she'd give me a little slap on the back of my head, say, "*Pobre viejita,*" ‡ make the sign of the cross, and forbid me from leaving the house with wet hair, in that order.

Ever since I was a little kid, she also had a phobia of seeing me play with plastic bags, because of some story about my grand-mother's brother. Or one of my grandmother's neighbours' brother or maybe even his classmate. Or scenarios she made up in her head. But someone somewhere in the world must have died of asphyxia-tion from a plastic bag. Sometimes, just to get a rise out of her, I'd put my head inside a bag but leave space for some air to get in. I waited until she noticed me breathing noisily, as if from a lack of oxygen. She would scream, get agitated, panic, all this punctuated by *Dios mío.*§ I'd stop just before it wasn't funny anymore. Then she'd let out a relieved but nervous laugh that belied a mix of reassurance, lightness, and profound distress. My mother's laughter: anxious joy at the end of a torment. I always found this nervous shift amusing.

I never noticed it in the mothers of my friends from here.

---

* Friends of Jesus.

† Fifteenth-birthday celebration.

‡ "Poor old lady."

§ My God.

Despite everything, I never questioned the truth of her stories. She believed in them, and this gave them a performative power over her. Madame Sepúlveda could very well think that it was because of her hair that her daughter had caught pneumonia, and my mother, that I could really die by getting my head caught in a plastic bag. It was their reality, not mine. They could fret all they liked, whether it was winter or summer, I never dried my jet-black hair before leaving the house. The only thing that killed me a little bit every day was to never see hair like mine anywhere but at the Latin American church or in front of my own mirror.

Book of the Month Club

NO SKIS, NO SNOWSHOES, NO HOCKEY, NO SKATES. WE BARELY
slid down a hill on a Crazy Carpet once a year. As soon as November
got here, we didn't do anything outside anymore and we became a
family of recluses. Except we'd chosen to live in a city of extreme
cold and abundant snow, where boredom in January was tolerable
but became unbearable by March.

Even if my mother's rough red hands were busy cleaning houses,
the educator in her refused to give up the ghost when it came to
her kids. She couldn't afford to pay for extracurricular activities for
us yet; that would come later. But she was determined to find us
some leisure activities that were more stimulating than television.
She got the idea to bring us to the library on Ontario Street, which
was free. If she couldn't bring us to the theatre—which she loved—
to watch the plays they put on for kids, she'd at least buy us bus
tickets for our weekly pilgrimage to the Hochelaga-Maisonneuve
Municipal Library.

The first time we went there as a family, I wasn't expecting to reel with amazement. I'd imagined a shabby sort of place, like everything else in the neighbourhood; instead, I found myself in front of the most beautiful building I'd ever seen in Montreal. I will remain convinced for the rest of my days that these places have to be beautiful to let us know they matter. This place was a palace, and as we went inside, even if the children's section was in the neon-lit basement, I felt I was gaining access to a treasure trove destined for me.

The library resembled a cathedral, majestic with its stone columns and many stairs to climb. The building had first been constructed to house Maisonneuve City Hall, not us kids from the hood. It was a hundred years old; only in 1980 had it become a library, the first sanctuary my mother showed us (although she did bring us to the Latin American church every Sunday).

We returned every Saturday, and the librarian soon got to know me and my tastes and began putting books aside for me. She offered me books that were a bit heftier, a bit more challenging than what I was used to reading, guiding me off the beaten paths, pulling me, one novel at a time, to a higher level. It was in this public library, between the bums who came to read the newspaper on comfortable sofas and the lonely women who came to escape the tedium of their lives, that I learned to rummage around among the various cultural offerings by myself. It was here that I borrowed a cassette of Gilles Vigneault's[57] songs, and poems by Félix Leclerc,[58] that I watched films by Marcel Pagnol[59] on VHS one rainy afternoon, that I read my first *Mafalda*[60] comic books and was astounded to learn that they were translations, and that the heroine was South American, like me.

The municipal library cleared a path of yearning for me; I embarked on it unaware that at the end, a new possibility awaited me, a multitude of paths different from the one I'd thought was necessarily my fate.

My mother might have intuited as much, but it wasn't enough to satisfy her. Rather, she regretted everything she couldn't offer us. She wished she could buy me all the books I obsessively borrowed (charming the librarian so she wouldn't object to me going over the limit). So that not just the stories would stay with me, but the actual, physical copies of the book too. The smell of old books would always remain a source of comfort to me; for my mother, it reminded her of her inability to give us everything we wanted.

As soon as she could afford it, she took out a subscription to Québec Loisirs, a book-of-the-month club. I remember the stranger who knocked on our apartment door, his mullet, his black jacket, his warm, hoarse, reassuring voice. He had kind eyes, so my mother let him come in. He sat down at the kitchen table, eagerly accepting the instant coffee she served him. I remember he cleared his throat before starting to speak, as if he was getting ready to reveal a secret. I remember he was gentle and confident and had silver rings that clinked against each other when he finally put down his little black fake-leather briefcase on the table. He opened it, and there were books inside. Hardcover books, with embossed titles. One catalogue per season; this was our spring.

In a long, well-rehearsed monologue, he introduced the club, which proposed books at discounted prices to be sent every month. There were deals like buy two, get one free. You could choose the books from the catalogue that came in the mail four times a year; there were bestsellers, books from obscure publishers, non-fiction, romance novels, biographies, historical novels. Once in a while, a Goncourt[61] slipped in, but most of the time they stuck to pop psychology and true stories. Put it this way: this was more like Consumers Distributing with books than l'Euguélionne.[62]

Over the seasons, my mother brought a lot of books into the house in addition to signing up friends and women from her church, and the club rewarded her with extra books. This was the club's heyday. As soon as the catalogue arrived at our house, we put on music, sat on the living room rug, circled titles with a red felt marker like with grocery flyers, and patiently waited for the mailman. I remember the boundless joy I felt upon receiving my own copy of *Les catastrophes de Rosalie*,[63] which I must have reread twenty times, and my first *Ani-Croche*.[64] There had always been joy at our house. From that day on, there were also books everywhere.

As we climbed the social ladder, the size of our apartments grew a little bit with each move. My mother decorated each new home with a few more books. An apartment would never be completely filled with books, but there were enough to cover part of the family room carpet, where I used to loll around, beside my mother and her nervous joy.

After a few years, my enthusiasm for my mother's book club faded. At the dawn of adolescence, after I'd read all the *Babysitter's Club* books, all the Lucy Maud Montgomerys and the Arlette Coustures,[65] I began to look at the club's other titles, the erotic books and the airport books, with some embarrassment. I was no longer sure this was the best way to obtain books. When I got to high school, five minutes of poetry was all it took for me to begin to scorn Québec Loisirs. By the time I was fourteen, I was outright ashamed of it.

I was talking on the phone with my best friend when my mother, looking completely thrilled, arrived in the living room with the winter catalogue. I quickly took in the cover: a huge close-up of the latest Danielle Steel with a bright blue book jacket and blazing golden letters: *Our favourite picks*. Before she could even say a word, I told her, "There's nothing but crap in that thing." I left the room quickly; I didn't wait to catch her look of disappointment. I left her, crushed, with her unsophisticated literature.

Even though I was no longer interested, my mother kept renewing her subscription for years. In addition to occasional novels, she completed her collection of books on biology, anatomy, illnesses, and medicine, as well as medical dictionaries. In her youth she had dreamed of becoming a pharmacist, but she'd gotten married at nineteen, fallen pregnant at twenty, lived under a dictatorship from the age of twenty-two, and erased the idea of herself in a white lab coat around the same time.

I didn't realize the health books she was accumulating in her little library continued to reveal her aborted dreams. As I turned into an adolescent, I stupidly constructed myself in reaction to her, against what she was made of, judging all that low and mediocre, scorning her culture, disdaining what she read. I didn't realize it was precisely because she had put so much effort into raising me that I could now look down on her.

Yet she was the one who both gave me my first language and put me on the path to distance myself from it. As those books piled up, another language began to stand between us. The language of the authorities, of the customs officials, of social services, of the school, of her bosses' orders. I began to read poetry and participate in literary contests at my school. The language that oppressed my mother was, from that point on, my new playground.

Do you know how to plant cabbages?[66]

WHEN I STARTED HIGH SCHOOL, MY PARENTS MOVED UP IN society and triumphantly left our Hochelaga-Maisonneuve apartment for a home in the suburbs. It was just a semi-detached house located in the B's, not in the S's, like where the nouveaux riches of Brossard lived, but anyway, they'd succeeded in leaving the concrete of the city behind for the southern suburbs, where they became homeowners. No more worrying about making too much noise for the downstairs neighbours or being disturbed by the ones upstairs. No more landlord to call to beg for a necessary repair: they finally didn't depend on anyone anymore.

Our neighbours to the right were courteous francophone labourers who managed to never speak to us; the Portuguese anglophile workers who lived to the left of us would greet us with exaggerated enthusiasm. Everyone had kids; they never would have ended up in the B's in Brossard otherwise. Our houses were almost identical, and all the kids were about the same age, but being teenagers, none were really friends. This didn't matter, since, for the first

time on Québécois soil, we had a yard, even if we shared it with
the Portuguese family; a row of cedars conveniently separated our
lawns, assuring us the privacy that came with moving up in the
world. The first afternoon we swam in our own above-ground pool,
which took up our whole side of the yard, we knew that our days of
destitution were behind us.

However, every spring brought that fateful moment when the
precariousness of our social station came back to haunt us. At winter's end, our neighbours would spread manure over their garden to
reinvigorate it. They grew tomatoes, lettuce, and cucumbers, like a
lot of South Shore families, but they also added those 1990s classics:
bell peppers, string beans, cabbage, and eggplants—in *Portuguese*
quantities. My parents could not understand this. Growing vegetables was for poor people. "*¡Cuando uno tiene un poco de plata,
se compran las legumbres en el negocio!*" * my father said between
clenched teeth as he closed the patio door. To say my parents hated
this is an understatement: they were mortified.

My mother had grown up with chickens in her yard. Not two
or three cute chickens called Gertrude like some hippies might
have up in Rosemont. Nor like the Cégep teacher who lives in
the countryside and keeps a chicken coop there, or like the urban-
hipster-turned-organic-farmer. Dozens of free-roaming chickens
in the yard, making a racket, pecking the seeds scattered over the
dirt and pebbles, leaving their feathers and their shit everywhere
they went. This was not at all a bucolic image for my mother; rather,
it represented cacophony, dirt, the stink of deprivation and need.
The scent of misery. Would she never be free?

Manure day was when it hit the hardest. The odour was an
annual reminder of our in-between status, of how our social ascen-
sion was also semi-detached. My parents may have become sub-
urban homeowners, but their neighbours grew immigrant vegetables
in their own semi-communal yard; it made the whole house smell

* "When you have a bit of money, you go to the store for your
vegetables!"

like shit and they couldn't do anything about it. The smell of manure like a stigma.

They talked about it for a week, closing all the windows, condemning themselves to the lives of recluses. "How much money can they be saving? Fifty dollars? A hundred?" Working all summer "like Chinese people" to save a hundred dollars for vegetables was inconceivable for my parents, who always ended their rant with "¡*Mentalidad de campesinos!*" * Of course, it did occur to them that gardening could well be a hobby and not just a question of need, but not the way our Portuguese friends did it: their vegetable plots had desperate proportions, like Russian *dachas*.

The cabbages our neighbours offered us were undoubtedly the most hated in all of Montérégie, and they invariably ended up in the garbage. Before even touching them, my mother knew they would taste of bitterness and betrayal. As if lurking behind the promise of every new summer was the requirement that she swallow her pride and slowly submit to the vengeance of her social class, hidden not all that far away, in the pit of her stomach.

---

* "Peasant mentality!"

Madame Brossard from Brossard [67]

THE FIRST TIME I WENT TO A SOCIOLOGY CLASS AT CÉGEP, IT was like hearing my mother tongue. It wasn't the only language that spoke of reality, nor even the best, but it was the one I recognized as my own. The language of sociology named things like social classes, exploitation, cultural, social, and symbolic capital. It especially talked about domination, but also, in its better moments, exorability, a possibility of escaping one's assumed lot in society. They were putting my reality into words. Long before I began my studies, I'd understood that our trajectories generally depended on where we were on society's chessboard. I knew what my place was and what was realistic for me to envisage in terms of social mobility.

I must have been seventeen, and like a perfect girlfriend, I often went to meet my boyfriend at his Cégep. He went to Brébeuf. [68] Not me, of course. I had to take the No. 5 bus on Grande-Allée to go to the bus terminal. We just called it the Brossard terminal, but it was really called Panama, which wasn't much better. The No. 45 bus left from there and crossed the Champlain Bridge [69] to get to

Montreal. If there wasn't much traffic, I'd have time to read one chapter of a book. Otherwise, I could read a few more, forty minutes' worth, in an accordion bus. At least I could see the river out the window. The 45 stopped at Place Bonaventure, and I'd take the metro from there to get to Snowdon station ten or fifteen minutes later. I then changed from the Orange Line to the Blue to get to Côte-des-Neiges, and from there walked toward Mont Royal. That was the last and, it seemed to me, longest step to gain access to private school culture.

I finally arrived at the top of the mountain, into a world whose symbolic violence leapt out at me. The shiny cars and the unfailingly clean shoes of those who got out of them. The immaculate, matching pastel clothes. The girls with their ballerina posture, the ease with which the boys spoke, their straight teeth and their private school accents. Their curious intellects, their rich vocabulary. Their grace, the relaxed stance of their bodies. Heads with real haircuts, discreet jewellery, flawless skin. Bodies rid of excess hair by efficient and long-lasting methods. Hands without imperfections, nails without dirt. Brands on their clothes, no marks on their skin. The unshakable confidence they had that the world belonged to them. How right they were.

I studied at Édouard-Montpetit, the Cégep closest to my house. To my boyfriend's friends, I wasn't a real Montrealer but a suburbanite. They joked that I was "Madame Brossard de Brossard," erasing my origins: the fact that I'd lived most of my life in Montreal, in the poorest neighbourhoods, and especially the fact that I had not been born here. I wasn't thrilled about this; I took it as an insult, even worse than when people thought I didn't speak French because of the colour of my skin. They made it seem as if our difference was a matter of personal choice, of school, not of class and even less so of race, as if at their level it didn't matter anymore. They spoke in universal terms, as if our experiences were similar and our cultures identical.

But it was clear that I wasn't one of them. Sure, I could date one of them, hang around with them for hours, speak their language, but everything kept bringing me back to those gaps that separated us. When they talked about their family vacations to Paris, their tennis lessons, the last play their mother had brought them to see at Espace Go,[70] the croissants from the Pâtisserie de Gascogne, the pretty girls from Villa Maria, their former rivals from Mont-Saint-Louis, their next ski weekend with their friends, sushi for lunch, their favourite Scotch at their grandfather's place, of Émile Ajar, Peter Handke, and the intrinsic qualities of *Journey to the End of the Night* despite its author being a Nazi, the gap grew deeper. I saw myself on the other side of an increasingly deep trench while they were far ahead, farther than I could glimpse.

Even when I'd spent an hour getting ready, nothing brilliant came out of my mouth, my dull hair was a mess of tangles, and my clothes seemed cheap. I never managed to resolve the enigma and kept asking myself how they managed to be so relaxed and sure of being in their rightful place. The same feeling seized me when I heard them arguing about foreign politics as if it were a game, a sort of mock oratory sword fight that had no effect on people's daily lives, a theoretical pleasure without consequences for real human beings. In fact, they weren't wrong; none of what they discussed had any impact on them or their opportunities, their future an immense and clear horizon that stretched out before them. I refrained from saying anything. We were so far apart that they could not perceive even a whisper of my reality.

The world that had birthed them was the same one that nourished class domination, and this world spoke louder, over everyone else. I felt a cold rush of fear when I realized, on my way back on the bus, that if I climbed this social ladder, I would undoubtedly take on the dominant side's judgments, their mores, and their ways of thinking.

Going the opposite way on the 45, heading home to my parents, I realized it would be impossible for me to disavow the world of my origins. This world was personified by my mother. She was the one who never stopped watching over me on these uncharted roads no one in the family had taken before me. She was the one who pointed out the obstacles, to prevent me from losing my footing. She held my hand at the crossroads even when I was distancing myself from my origins. She was the one holding the signs and balloons at every finish line, even though each of them signalled departures from my community. Because it was my mother, who sacrificed every single one of her days and several of her nights to see me liberated from her life of servility and submission, who most wanted to see me succeed. Because she prayed—on her knees to the Virgin Mary in every chapel—that I manage to escape and transcend my predetermined place in society. Because even if I was pitting myself against her and embracing the social codes that excluded her, I made her very proud. Because the betrayal required by this upward mobility was not only expected but hoped for.

The 45 was always full on my trip home and it wasn't unusual for me to have to stand for the whole journey. It was a long way getting there and even longer coming back.

Toward the end of the winter session, at the very beginning of one of the long trips that took me to the hilltops of Brébeuf, I was feeling weary of reading *The Tin Flute*,[71] which I'd been carrying around with me for a week. I began to observe the people around me. Only white people, except the bus driver, who was Asian, and me. I looked up and my eyes landed on a series of ads for a *francisation* school for adult immigrants. The kind of ad that features racialized people, all smiles, with straight white teeth, looking fresh and tidy, never tired. People who look like young professional actors from various ethnic groups, or French expats, wearing under-eye concealer, rather than workers from Parc-Ex who send half their pay home to their families in Peru or in Haiti.

Each of these ads presented a different sort of immigrant with their reason for attending the classes above their photo. These were often very pragmatic, like "To get a good job." An effective bit of advertising with a closely targeted audience. As I examined them, one of the ads struck me hard. It showed an unsmiling Black man with straight, dignified shoulders and a frank, almost accusing expression on his face. It said, "So that one day I can tell you my story." My reaction surprised me: big, fat, unstoppable tears began to flow down my brown cheeks. I immediately recognized them: my mother's tears.

The tears that come with isolation, self-restraint, suffocation, indifference, the loss of identity, the shame of being who you are, invisible against the backdrop of a world that screams its joy at you, the joy of just existing.

It was on this bus, at the beginning of the trip that would bring me to Brébeuf, a private school I didn't attend, that I promised myself that I would write. That what I wrote would be stark, powerful, and violent, as if my ancestors, those who'd been sacrificed, the anonymous ones left behind, could read over my shoulder. Write as if the women who'd preceded me were rising from beneath the earth to watch me. All the women. The fat ones, the starving ones, the prostitutes, the pious, the illiterate, the screamers, the damned, the insane, the abandoned, the hags, the mute, the gossips, the alcoholics, the virgins, the Sibyls, the psychics, the blind, the diminished, the sassy ones, the beaten ones, the angry ones, the crying, the heaving, the raped, the sorrowful, the stooped, the beauties, the offended ones, the ones in pain, the uncrushable ones, the tortured, the lionesses, the bitches, the depressed, the ones people avoided, the submissive ones, the shrews, the crushed, the fairies, the mothers, *las Negras*, *las brujas*,* and the damned.

My writing would be like a *danse macabre* or a cry of revolt. Like a whole supper dropped on the floor when food is scarce. Like a primal scream in response to a sexual assault. Like the disappearance of a child after the coup d'état. Like a decade of dictatorship over all of Latin America. Like the silent tears in the basements where you sit praying. I would write my story, like all these women in me who must be brought back to life.

---

* The Black ones, the witches.

Love is in your eyes tonight[72]

WHEN WE MOVED TO THE SOUTH SHORE, WE ACQUIRED A
new kind of friend, the kind whose parents go away for a few days.
It isn't that they disappear or abandon their kids. No, these parents
leave on business trips, on romantic weekends, to the cottage for a
long weekend, and they leave the house in their teenagers' care with
the aim of teaching them to be responsible.

Of course, mine never left. Or if they did, they brought us
along. When we went away, it was the five of us together, with a
Dunkin' Donuts thermos filled with filter coffee and a cooler full
of hard-boiled eggs for the long drive. The only time my mother
left without us for a few days was for her father's funeral. It never
occurred to my parents to have some time alone together, or just
some time off alone.

But my friends' parents were neither immigrants nor Latinos.
They went away from time to time; they always left food in the
fridge. All my friends, without exception, jumped on these occasions to host parties. Sometimes it was just a few kids hanging out,

a group of four or five. We made punch by mixing several ounces of each kind of alcoholic beverage we found in the house. It was, without fail, completely disgusting, and we drank it quickly just to get drunk, even when it tasted like ass. More rarely, we lost control, and the little party became an open house where friends of friends invited their acquaintances. We'd suddenly find ourselves with dozens of strangers and blaring music in a house on one of those empty streets on the South Shore.

We generally had a party to go to every Friday, especially since the guys in our gang had introduced their hockey friends to us. These kids went to different private schools: Charles-LeMoyne, Durocher, or Collège Français.

This one time, the host was one of the guys from Jean de la Mennais. I didn't know anything about him, except that he lived in La Prairie and had invited us over on a Thursday night, which was unusual. His parents had left for their country home that morning; they'd given themselves a long Thanksgiving holiday to enjoy the autumn colours. In those days I didn't understand what people did near a lake that was too cold to swim in. A white-people thing, I told myself as I set off with my friend Gen to this boy's house. A boy I knew only by his hockey nickname: Beauty.

As always, when we went to the home of a boy we didn't know and rang the doorbell, our excitement overcame our misgivings. Our host didn't answer the door; he was too busy serving tequila shooters. Instead, it was our friend JF who came to greet us. There were already about fifteen people inside, but for some reason, despite the open cases of beer all over the place, there was something heavy about the atmosphere. Some guys were playing video games, others a bit farther off played guitar, and a few others played foosball. A few girls served as an audience; they lay sprawled out on the sofas watching the boys. Blink 182 was singing "Wasting Time," but these people were not talking to each other, and when they did, they whispered. Things were just too controlled.

Though we'd just come in, a strange feeling took hold of me. Everything was spinning around, as if I was already drunk. I felt heavy and breathless. I felt as if I had got caught in a trap of my own making. I wished I could lie down on the ground, roll myself up in the Moroccan rug, close the blinds. It felt like someone had reshuffled a deck of cards and I was suddenly buried under the rubble of my memories. And I had a palpable sense that something was about to happen.

I felt I had to leave. But I gradually began to distrust that feeling. Was it because it was a Thursday? Because I hadn't told my parents that I was going to a party but that I was sleeping over at Gen's house? Because Gen already had a beer in her hand, and she was the one driving? Because there was a ratio of four boys to one girl? I had my period; maybe I was just a bit light-headed.

My gaze zigzagged from one piece of furniture to the next in the heavy, baroque decor before it decided to settle on something: a boy. Beauty was the only person who looked like he was having fun. Every time someone bit into a slice of lemon, he burst out laughing. His laughter crackled; it was crystal clear and sincere, spilling over like a child's. He didn't know it, but he immediately calmed me down. He stood up, and I was able to observe his body, from far away. His wide shoulders. He was tall, with the posture of a guy who had taken music lessons and had had a secure childhood. He moved minimally and gently, without a trace of aggression. He ran his fingers coquettishly through the waves of his light brown hair. I felt him slipping under my skin when he rolled up the sleeves of his sweater. My heart turned to mush as I caught sight of the veins along his forearms.

I still had my coat on and my eyes glued on Beauty when my friend JF put his hand on my shoulder.

"You're really pale. Are you all right?"

"Yeah, my stomach hurts a little, but I'm okay."

"Anyway, I'm glad you're here. This party's a bit lame."

"It *is* quiet. Did something happen?"

"No, maybe this house is like, just too big… Is Véro coming?"

My friend Véro worked until eight-thirty. She was the only person who could bring this party to life. Véro was sassy, a badass.

Her casual insolence always spurred people to interact, and even sparked friendships. While I waited for her, I took off my coat to go introduce myself to the guy I'd had my eye on. But when I got to the kitchen, he wasn't there anymore.

Someone was knocking on the door, desperately; it had to be Véro, who never rang the bell. JF made her wait, knowing it would make her furious. Before he opened the door, I had time to drink a tequila shooter, lick up the salt, bite into the piece of lemon, and hear Beauty say in a bright, hoarse voice that went straight to my gut, "Okay, let's get this party started!" He put on "Santeria" by Sublime.

Véro came in swearing. I was right; as soon as she stepped inside the door, she'd sensed the weight of the waning small talk. She opened her army surplus shoulder bag, took out a big bottle of Tornade she'd already started, chugged down the rest without even taking off her *tuque*, and then let out a huge, trucker-worthy belch as a general greeting to the crowd. She winked at me as she walked over to the stereo and, without asking anyone, removed the Sublime CD and replaced it with Cypress Hill. She cranked up the sound. She'd gotten what she wanted: everyone was looking at her.

"All right. What are we doing now? Shooters or bottles?"

I spotted Beauty. His profile revealed a straight, imperial nose, my favourite kind. He was smiling and listening distractedly. He was refilling bowls with Hostess chips, tasting each of the three kinds, one after another, taking the time to lick his index finger, his middle finger, and his thumb. He had piano-lesson fingers and large palms I thought were surely agile and patient. Before I lost my head imagining the eagerness of his mouth, I blurted out an answer.

"I'm game for the bottle!"

"Fuck, yeah!" Véro shouted as she put down her empty bottle of Tornade, without waiting for any other response.

A few guys pretended to balk. Not Beauty. He turned around, and I could finally see his face. The fine line of his jaw, his pink cheeks, his large mouth, half-open lips, his straight, post-braces teeth. He smiled, openly pleased with the suggestion, and he was even more good-looking than I'd imagined. Despite his hockey-player build, he wasn't the most masculine guy. Everything about him was delicate and gentle. Light, poised, airy, the opposite of aggressive. He was a dream.

The other guys didn't need to have their arms twisted; they took their places in the circle forming around the bottle of Tornade on the living room carpet as Beauty, who hadn't yet noticed me, uncapped one of my bottles of Molson Export and took a big swig. He was game too. A look of satisfaction, a little smile.

Determined to make this the most perfect moment ever, I took my Fugees CD out of my bag and chose "Killing Me Softly with His Song."

"Good call," Beauty said, turning to face me for the first time.

Lauryn Hill might have been singing, but the second his grey eyes dove into mine, all I could hear was a gulp in my own throat. There was something sad and dark deep in his eyes, the kind of look I always fall in love with. I held his attention, managed not to tremble, flinch, or collapse. As we looked into each other's eyes, I didn't hear the music anymore, and time slowed down. His gaze examined every cranny of my mind. My eyes moored in his. I smiled. I became at once prayer and fire. We absorbed each other.

Delighted, Beauty intercepted my prayers and laughed. He'd orchestrated this storm. He'd de-orbited me. My panicked eyes desperately wanted to get off at the next stop but didn't know how. The feeling had completely taken me over: this boy's eyes had penetrated me.

Where did this strong sense of déjà vu come from? My eyes fell on the solid wood cabinet, on the bookcase that went all the way to the ceiling, on the fireplace. I was suddenly and brutally certain that I'd been in this house before and that I'd already turned toward his November-grey eyes.

"No," I said aloud when I recognized where I was.

Beauty had just sat down across from me and was giving me a suave smile, as if we had all the time in the world to get to know each other. He didn't know, didn't recognize me.

"No. Fuck! No!" I said, getting up now, horrified.

No, fuck, no, I couldn't believe it, I'd already been here, as a little girl. It must have been a long time ago; the furniture had been moved around, the kitchen redone, the walls repainted, but the more I looked around, the more I knew I was in familiar territory: the samovar, the oak cabinet, the long staircase that led upstairs. Now I was sure: I was at a party, as if everything was normal, at one of the houses my mother had cleaned every Friday for years.

I'd seen Beauty when we were kids. He was my mother's client's only son. We had met on a pedagogical day when I'd tagged along with my mother. I'd brought my *Babysitters' Club* book, and I'd sat down across from him while he watched MusiquePlus on TV. We'd exchanged awkward hellos and then stayed there like that, him on the sofa, me on the loveseat, uncomfortable in our silence during the whole program, until he returned to his bedroom. At the last minute, just before he went up those stairs that were so hard to dust, he'd looked at me for a long time and then said, "Natalia's your mother, eh? You don't look like her."

I hadn't appreciated his verdict at the time and, my stomach in knots, I realized that this present version of Beauty had chosen to hold his party on a Thursday because my mother would be there the next day to clean up.

I began to look around in silence, imagining how my mother would see this place: The entrance covered in mud. All the bottles on the wooden table without coasters underneath them. The mountain of dishes accumulating in the sink. The slices of lemon everywhere, the salt on the floor. The windowpanes covered in fingerprints. It was only the beginning of the party, and I could already count six full garbage bags to take out.

I wished I could start cleaning up. Put the damn cigarillos out in the ashtrays. Empty them so my mother wouldn't have to touch the filthy things the next day. I wished I could clean everything before some drunk girl vomited her Tornade, or someone spilled a beer, or broke a glass. I wished I could stop the music. How come Cypress Hill was back on again? What were they all doing, listening to Cypress Hill when there were no Latinos, much less Black people, in the house?

I picked up my Molson, as well as Beauty's, and went to put them in the empty case. I did my best to wipe up the drops on the floor with my sleeve.

"What are you doing?" Beauty asked. "Just leave that."

As if I needed one last confirmation, I looked at his ash-coloured eyes. Yes, it was him. He had his mother's eyes.

"I have to go."

"What, already? The party's just started."

"I have to go home. I'm not feeling well."

As if he'd read my mind, he went back to the stereo and turned off "Boom Biddy Bye Bye" right in the middle of the chorus that some guys clearly knew by heart and were happily singing along to. While the others were playing spin the bottle, Beauty replaced the CD with *The Bends* by Radiohead and chose the track "High and Dry." He started dancing with big, expansive moves—as did my heart. Grey eyes, a bit of attention, sad boy music, that's all it took to make me swoon. An embrace wasn't far away; I had to leave before I kissed him. Sensing that I was trying to slip away, he walked over, took a stray lock of my hair, and delicately replaced it behind my ear.

"Come on, let's go upstairs. It'll be quieter," he whispered, tenderly lacing my fingers in his.

I knew exactly where his bedroom was: second floor, second door on the left, across from one of the three bathrooms. I remembered his hockey cards scattered everywhere on his bedside table when he was a child. The yellow Walkman he always left lying on the floor. The Ninja Turtles poster that adorned his bedroom door. The unfailingly sticky doorknob my mother had wiped every Friday, for years. The doorknob my mother would wipe again the next day.

I shook my head. For the last time, I looked deeply into his eyes. They were as infinitely vast as a romantic disappointment.

I slipped my hand out of his and went to the door. I tidied the shoes on the straw mat, wiped the floor with my mitten, but

I left the rest for my mother: the overflowing ashtrays, the empty bottles and the bottle caps everywhere, the broken chips on the carpet, the bits of cheese on the floor, the little baggies of weed on the counter, the rolling papers on the table, the glasses, the tons of glasses everywhere, glasses that would fill the dishwasher, the paper towels soaked with spilled alcohol, the smell of vanilla cigarillos that settles in and takes hours of fanning to dissipate, the bathrooms, the fucking bathrooms where dozens of people had gone to piss.

I left. I left Beauty behind. Gen followed me. She was a good friend. She didn't bombard me with questions. "Wait, he gave me this for you," she said as she fished her car keys out of her bag to bring me home. I unfolded the slip of paper she was holding out to me. A phone number.

Nobody had a cellphone at that time. It was the home phone. The same number from which his mother called mine to cancel when the family was off on a ski trip and my mother found herself involuntarily on holiday. I sighed, folded the paper, and, once inside the car, flipped through Gen's CDs. I quickly found *The Bends*, put it on ("Nice Dream"), closed my eyes, and leaned my head against the window as my friend drove me home. I wished there was a storm, but it wasn't even raining. Everything was dry and the trees we passed were magnificent with their autumn colours, standing straight, impassive, and majestic.

I kept the number in a pocket of my jeans for three days. Then my mother picked my jeans off my messy bedroom floor to put them in the wash. The paper came back to me crumpled, illegible, useless.

Eat your socks[73]

MY MOTHER AND I WERE ON EITHER SIDE OF THE KITCHEN counter, as was our habit when I didn't have any classes before the end of the afternoon. My mother's day had started much earlier. She'd had the time to go clean a house, return, begin one part or another of our supper, and confront the chores from our own house, alone. It was across this counter that we had our most important conversations, without necessarily ever looking at each other. She busied herself at the oven, with the dishes, or with cleaning the house; I would sit, eating my toast, my eggs, a glass of orange juice in my hand, doing some last-minute reading for one of my university courses, studying Russian declensions, distractedly reading *Le Devoir* while complaining about provincial politics. How bittersweet it must have been for her to see me both emancipated and so indifferent to her reality.

One day, I sat in a cloud of garlic and sautéed onions, going through my notes for my course on Rawls when I noticed she had a run in her stockings. She was always perfectly turned out. She'd taught me how to repair my own stockings by applying transparent nail polish on them. So I told her so she could take care of them as soon as possible. While she was taking her nail polish out of the fridge, I remembered a story my friend had told me. It was the kind of syrupy, sentimental story that had been going around for years before it reached my ears. Whether or not it was true, I'd found it beautiful, and I repeated it to my mother while she took care of her stocking.

"I don't know if this really happened, but a friend told me that noblewomen used to wear stockings under their skirts. Lovely thick white stockings. They were luxury items, expensive underthings that poor women couldn't afford but found a way to imitate. They shaved their legs and painted them white. It created something like the smooth, thick texture of the stockings, you know, which they couldn't afford. And that's supposedly where the idea of shaving our legs came from. Incredible, eh?"

My mother's face changed. Her good mood suddenly dissipated, leaving a melancholy that gently but irrepressibly overwhelmed her. She looked away before her eyes almost imperceptibly filled with water. The silence was heavy. I had trouble understanding what had happened. I didn't say anything, not wanting to disturb my gentle and sensitive mother. We could still hear the onions crackling in the pan, but my mother went mute. The only sounds to fill the silence resounding in the room were of Fiori,[74] Garou,[75] and Lavoie[76] singing "Belle" on the radio. The song was of a violent impertinence. And interminable.

My mother continued to go about her chores as if nothing was wrong. I didn't take my eyes off her; I followed her movements, from the sink to the stove, from the stove to the fridge, from the fridge to the garbage can. I sensed her suffer as she made the kitchen the theatre of her restraint; I saw her tremble, control herself, and scrub as if her life depended on it. Then, holding the lid of the garbage can in one hand, she abruptly turned toward me and told me in French, in one breath so she wouldn't cry: "If I had lived in those times, I would have been one of those poor people. I would have had to shave my legs. Paint them. I wouldn't have had any nylons."

While women have always made use of subterfuge to conform to ridiculous ideals of beauty, the ideals themselves remained inaccessible to my mother and her like. Although my mother was very beautiful, she was one of those girls who had to improvise her own tricks to follow fashion. When she was eighteen—the age I was when I told her that stupid story about the stockings—she used old scissors to curl her eyelashes. She recycled old lipsticks to use as blush. She smoothed her hair with saliva. She used nails to knit clothes that almost resembled the ones she saw in shop windows; she never actually entered those shops. Even if the story of the shaven legs painted white was a complete invention, it was about her, about this young girl with the knobby knees and the languid air that never left her.

I should have known: my mother's reflex would always be to see herself in the role of the naughty girl in retreat, in a world that rendered her servile. That would forever be my mother's deeply held vision of herself. She may have been the owner of a pretty house in Brossard, two cars, a garage, and an above-ground pool, but my mother always felt more rags than riches. She related better to homeless people who had to swallow their pride and eat their socks. Her childhood had assigned her this place, and that's where she would always reside. That is the part of herself that has stayed the same.

Furor[77]

QUÉBEC, LIKE ALL PLACES THAT TAKE IN NEWCOMERS, LIKES
to present refugees as success stories: talk about the international
conflicts that made them victims, contrast that with our model of
integration, and then triumphantly point to the success of all the
Michaëlle Jeans,[78] Kim Thúys,[79] and Dany Laferrières.[80] Highlight
the success of those who became doctors, those who are now lawyers.

We never hear of what happened to the ordinary refugees
struggling through shit in Rivière-des-Prairies, or worse, the failed
refugees. We don't talk about them; they don't exist. We don't talk
about the silent refugees.

What happened to the other children in Madame Thérèse's
class? Maybe the little Turkish kid is picking cigarette butts up off
the ground. Or empty cans from the sidewalk on avenue Coloniale
on recycling day. Maybe the Haitian girl, now forty years old, is
childless and still partying at the Salsathèque or at Balattou, collecting fuchsia dresses and one-night stands. The Salvadorian
might be working at the factory, watching *Sábado Gigante*[81] on his

special international cable channel and spending his weekends in an alcoholic funk. And the integrated Kurd is doing the same thing with his lukewarm Labatt 50 and *La poule aux œufs d'or.*[82]

I have no idea. Most likely, the majority live in suburbia with its 1.88 birth rate, listening to the roar of *Paw Patrol* with their children while making a grocery list for Super C. Like everyone else.

So, by the time I got to Cégep, I seemed to fit in. I'd learned the language, I said yes, I said thank you, I swore parsimoniously and at the right time. I never asked for anything, worked my ass off at school the way my parents applied themselves to cleaning bathrooms. So perfect I had no accent, debts, liabilities, or recriminations. I never turned anything down, never balked at anything. A job, a friend, an invitation, a piece of advice, an order, a contemptuous comment, an insult, two million humiliations. I never let anyone glimpse the anxious confusion and hate behind my smiles, the insecurity that shrouded my nights. I disappeared into the crowd—I had the same values, the same clothes, the same references, and I pretended to have the same history. Model student, high expectations, impeccable grooming, rich vocabulary, a sense of community. Years of having the sole obsession of belonging had resulted in me becoming an exemplary immigrant. A fucking model of integration.

Very late one night following a storm, I was at Foufounes Électriques listening to Vilain Pingouin[83] and trying to attract the attention of a local star when I glanced at my phone and stopped breathing. I'd just started university and one of my high school friends had put an end to his life. He'd suffocated himself with a plastic bag. Even if I didn't recite the rosary like my mother, I cried so much that I would swear on the heads of my ancestors that the Saint-Laurent swelled its banks.

I suppose you could say that that's when I really became Québécoise: before I turned twenty, when, like everyone else, I had a friend who had committed suicide.

Time of the Buffoons[84]

I WAS STUDYING SOCIOLOGY AT UNIVERSITÉ DE MONTRÉAL when one of my leftist classmates and I started a political film festival. We invited Pierre Falardeau[85] to come and present *Time of the Buffoons*, which we'd dusted off for the occasion. Falardeau had filmed the bicentennial banquet of the Beaver Club, a private club founded by fur traders, showing the colonial bourgeoisie dancing and eating, dressed in the new clothes of domination. After the screening, he discussed colonialism and sovereignty with the hundred or so enthralled young adults present.

As a member of the organizing committee, I had the opportunity to join him and a few associates for the drink he'd readily agreed to. I sat next to him in the bar's basement.

A few years earlier, Falardeau had published an essay entitled *"La liberté n'est pas une marque de yogourt."** It became the topic of discussion as a second round of pints was served. This was followed

---

* Liberty is not a brand of yogourt.

by a long discussion on Québec independence, where we clearly were not all in agreement: some people were reformists, others Black Bloc anarchists. As U of M attracted few leftists, we often found ourselves sitting around the same table without killing each other. Some of my friends began an interminable and raucous debate on the best ways to create a real revolution. The kind of exchange that signals the end of the evening and is annoying to everyone except two or three insufferable dudes who name themselves the people's comrades and ceaselessly rehash the same arguments whenever they have an audience. Taking advantage of Pierre Falardeau's irritated silence, as well as our proximity to one another, I got the bright idea of telling him my own story, the one about the little refugee who spotted a container of Liberté yogourt for the first time. Today, I wonder what came over me. I now find it as hilarious as it was insane to have chosen Pierre Falardeau to be the first person to hear such a personal story.

I told him the whole thing: our journey as asylum seekers, our confinement at the hotel, our stay with the Chilean family. I talked about my appetite and yearning, about the yogourt, about freedom, and especially about my shame. He listened patiently until the end. His gaze seemed attentive, his eyes lively; he appeared moved. When I was done, he put his hand on my knee, lightly and with kindness. Then, with a mischievous, mocking smile, he removed it and said with nonchalance, "Well, that little story of yours is pretty pathetic!"

I didn't know what to say. It must have been one in the morning, I'd just spilled my guts to a key figure in Québec society, this man whom I'd respected, and he just dismissively ridiculed my life and mocked my vulnerabilities.

"Wow, fuck you, man." Those are the only words that occurred to me to say to Pierre Falardeau, icon of Québécois cinema. He didn't say anything for a moment, and then he burst out laughing, a long, cascading laugh, his eyes sparkling again.

I was so offended I couldn't follow the conversation after that. I was finally roused from my torpor when everyone started singing "The Mysterious Cities of Gold."

Since my teens, almost all the men I'd been with had talked to me about one of the well-known characters on that show, the enigmatic Zia. I think they stupidly imagined they'd find something of her in me, like a key to an exoticized El Dorado, an accomplice for the most exciting adventure of their lives. They must have been disappointed. Though they should have guessed that at the age when I was furiously changing the TV channel as soon as I heard "Children of the Sun," I was more like the monkey-faced Tao than Zia with her secrets and her silence.

Still, my university friends remember the famous Cities of Gold with nostalgia and cite the program as a key childhood influence. I don't know how many times, while in the midst of a battle against the Summit of the Americas, at meetings turned into leftist parties, some wise guy began to go, "Ahhhh ahhh ahhh ahhh...," and launch into wishing for the Cities of Gold. I don't know how many times I sang along with them in the early hours of the morning, though my inner child, who really was more like Tao, was exhausted and nauseated. Feeling betrayed once again, just wanting to leave.

This time, I looked at Falardeau, who didn't know the song. I told him, "It's a tune from their childhoods. I think they're nostalgic about colonization too."

If that poor guy knew that now when I see yogourt in my fridge, I think of him, rather than my first audacious act in this country! Doesn't matter the brand, or the size of the container, today it's that time I met him that's replaced my pathetic little story of liberty. I still resent him. Without meaning to, he stole my story and replaced it with his.

When I got back to my parents' place that weekend, I told my mother my whole story in abundant detail. She listened in silence, smiling and caressing my black hair with her worn hands, as she always did when I delivered monologues.

When I'd finished, she asked me: "*¿Quién es Pierre Falardeau?*" *

---

* Who is Pierre Falardeau?

The Quiet Revolution

USUALLY, AFTER DEMONSTRATIONS WITH THE ANARCHISTS, we'd go to Yer'mad to play foosball or to Café Chaos if we already knew we wanted to close the bar, our ears damaged. This time, I was with an eclectic group that brought together radical feminists from UQAM,[86] an old friend from the far left, but mostly people studying sociology and anthropology at Université de Montréal. There was one girl I liked who had a lot in common with all the students in that department: she was an enthusiastic, optimistic, white feminist, full of good intentions.

Following our annual March 8 march, just after a junkie told us, in front of his drunk girlfriend, that we needed a good fuck, we stopped at l'Amère à boire. Between two pints of blond, the anthropology student started to rant, "I will never understand why some women aren't feminists. Being a feminist is such a no-brainer. Even my great-grandmother, you could say she was a feminist before her time—well, at least she didn't let the priest tell her how many kids she had to have. And my grandmother Jeannette was absolutely a feminist...like almost all women of her generation, no? She was one of Morgentaler's[87] early supporters! So, for me, you see, being a feminist, it was just obvious. Like for you, I imagine."

The violence of these glib remarks, her "no-brainer," had the same harsh effect on me as a stroboscope. Every one of her sentences a bright, obtrusive, intermittently flashing light. This belief that during the Quiet Revolution, everyone in Québec was ready. That everyone was naturally unfettered, liberated, and on the left. That this vision of history did not ignore the majority of those who live on its fringes. That it must be so validating to see yourself in the march of history, the one that's tracked and recorded and studied at school, the one you find in the textbooks, the one that expresses itself more often, and more articulately, and that leaves its mark.

The first time I felt as if a book talked about my family was when I read *Les Misérables*. That was when I understood misery was universal. When I was twenty, I read Victor Hugo and it struck me like a revelation. Hugo wrote about my grandmother's reality a century earlier, without ever having set foot in Chile. My mother's family had never heard of him.

The two stories are still linked together in my mind today. The images described by one superimpose themselves on the other. Every time someone mentions Victor Hugo's name, I think of my grandmother's tragic life: her childhood, marked by starvation and the cruelty of the lower depths of Latin American society, the way she was fated to age prematurely, the particularly deplorable lot in life accorded to her as a woman, everything that is engendered by privation, need, and the vexations of the soul.

My feminism doesn't come from a founding myth where my grandmother, in step with the liberal, educated women of her era, would have fought for the right to an abortion. I didn't inherit feminism by osmosis, I pulled it out of the earth; it was deeply buried beneath all the hopes and dreams and disappointments of the women in my family. Abortion is illegal in Chile and contraception is frowned upon. What would I have had to sacrifice, as a woman, had I remained there? Every move toward liberation, as imperceptible as it might be, weighed heavily on their consciences and on their lives, carrying their share of suffering and grief: my grandmother, who left her husband, my mother, her country. The older I get, the more I realize that they bore their quiet revolutions like penances.

My grandmother made just one misstep; she wore it like a stigmata and embodied the Confiteor for the rest of her life, convinced she would go to hell. They may have lived at the same time, but she had nothing in common with her sisters in Québec; a universe separated them.

I didn't say much to my friend. Only that my grandmother definitely didn't consider herself a feminist. And that she'd never fought for anything apart from her own survival.

For better or worse

ALMOST AS SOON AS I FINISHED MY STUDIES, I GOT THE JOB of my dreams. No longer the invisible child tagging along with her parents in deserted bank offices; that girl was far away now. I found my place on a revolving armchair: I became a sociology teacher in a Cégep. However, I've always had trouble seeing this as a job. I don't have a boss who could just show me the door tomorrow morning. It's not a job that gets my hands dirty or makes me keep my head down, it doesn't smell like dirty coffee machine filters, the plastic of water coolers, a mixture of Windex and bleach.

I've been teaching a course called "Sociologie du Québec" for about ten years. I talk about the Quiet Revolution, gender social-ization, changes in the suicide rate, integration into Québec society, institutional racism, and social classes. I teach the social codes of Québec with terms provided by sociology, as if these were my words. I'm paid to read, to write, to think, to speak in front of a class. Dozens of young, sharp eyes look at me, observe me. These young people listen to me explain *le vivre-ensemble*.* They listen as I reveal the importance of the social realm for human beings. Sociology gave me a voice.

As if that weren't enough, I've been able to have my voice heard all over the world. While on a trip to Lisbon, I met a tall, handsome Swede with whom I had a long-distance relationship for two years before we decided to get married. My mother, who dreamed her whole life of being a pharmacist, couldn't get over it: a blond, Scandinavian pediatrician as a son-in-law. In life's lottery, I'd won the husband jackpot.

I was returning from an umpteenth Atlantic crossing to spend a few weeks with my fiancé, and my parents, devoted as always, had come to pick me up at the airport. We were driving home, and I was telling them about his family—his father, who was also a doctor, and his mother, who came from Swedish nobility, dean of a law faculty—when my mother interrupted me: "But what does he see in you?"

You might think it incongruous for the knobby-kneed little girl in her to see the one I had become, but that would be to misunderstand my mother, who not only called me *mi reina*,† but who believed it. For many years now, I was no longer a little refugee in her eyes but a privileged, *bourgeoise* woman who lived an open, unconcealed life, who taught young Québécois students about their own society, who had the opportunity to travel all over the world, to afford a long-distance relationship, to drop her work for a while for the sake of her new love affair in Stockholm.

"But what does he see in you?" marked the distance between our class lines, which I had crossed, but which she also knew still lurked somewhere deep inside me. She wasn't questioning the legitimacy of my place. It was just that she knew I was less comfortable in a ball gown than surrounded by workers at rush hour in a packed

---

* Harmonious cohabitation between individuals or between communities.

† My queen.

metro. She knew that it was in a hot, crowded bus, listening to gossip and reading over shoulders, that I felt part of the collective. She knew it, but I didn't yet. A few months later, I left everything behind and went to live in Sweden.

And I nearly didn't come out of there alive.

I was expecting. Going through my first pregnancy relegated to the domestic sphere, in a country where I could only stammer a few words of the language, opened wounds. I had scars I wasn't even aware of. Despite my financial independence, despite my upward mobility, despite my culture, I couldn't cope. Being the Other again. Far from everything I had struggled so hard to make my own. To find myself once more anonymous and mute, in a city that was magnificent, wealthy, and cold. Once again, I didn't belong. Stockholm, my shining diamond, my ice palace, my bell jar.

I came back to Québec feeling petrified, wondering the same thing: "But what does he see in you?"

Now I know my ABCs

NOBODY SAID TO ME: FIND A WAY TO BE YOURSELF IN THIS body of yours, invent a way to combine French and Spanish instead of putting them in separate compartments. Instead, I understood the hierarchy of the elementary schoolyard, of the locker rooms at the municipal swimming pool, in the school bus, in the stores where I was followed from the age of twelve if they hadn't heard me speak French without an accent. I was sketchy.

We never stopped speaking our mother tongue at home, but as time went on, it took on a private quality, relegated to the family domain. My parents wanted their children to integrate. They wanted a better future for us, and that had to mean a certain detachment from our roots, an attenuation of whom we'd been. While we'd never renounce our origins, we learned to keep them within our family, in a secret, folkloric drawer, deep inside the domestic sphere.

After a few years, I stopped using Spanish except for the most banal, everyday conversation, the typical Latin American family negotiations—pass me the bread, no butter thanks, no, I'm not on a diet, stop saying that, I am *not* skinny, I'll be home late tonight, no, I'm sure it'll be later than that, yes, the girls will be there, no, there won't be any boys, we won't be drinking, yes, yes, I'll call. Trivialities and familiar phrases, never anything of significance.

The language I'd been rocked to sleep to as a child quickly became imprecise, fearful, and discreet. I spoke it at home, but it no longer served me well when I wanted to discuss the world I found myself in, my place in it, and how I thought about it. French replaced Spanish. I began to desert my mother tongue.

It got me back.

That's always the price to pay when moving from one social class to another. The place that becomes harder every day to return to. Today, when I hear my son speak French and Swedish perfectly, when I see him already interested in English but answering timidly and with a bit of annoyance when addressed in Spanish, I feel ashamed. Not of him: he welcomes these words with keenness and candour. Of me: I wasn't able to get over the embarrassment and stigma related to my mother tongue.

When he was three years old, he'd already understood that this language was inferior, something to be whispered. I'd hide it, mumble it, like a foreigner fearful of being unmasked, keep it secret between us to say we loved each other but also so we wouldn't be found. A language retreating to its lair. It's the only language for him not entirely synonymous with wonder and pride, and it's my fault, the fault of my history, my ratty immigrant baggage. I didn't know how to free his Spanish from the humiliations suffered in the past, from the contempt and the disgrace attached to it. My apprehension ended up dampening his enthusiasm, transforming Spanish into a language of anxiety, only hanging on by a thread.

I became aware of the terrible toll once I was an adult, when I had to put my newborn to bed. I heard my Swedish husband sing the songs his grandfather had sung to his father and that his father had sung to him. I had no lullabies to share from the opacity of my mother tongue. The Spanish lullabies had long since deserted my memory, slipped away. I'd neglected my own language and it turned furtive; without my realizing it, it had escaped me.

I looked up nursery rhymes and lullabies online, but I had to learn them by heart, artificially. The ones in French had never entirely belonged to me. If I knew them, it was because of television and because of my friends. I'd been a good audience, I'd heard them so much that they'd stuck to my memory, but I'd never experienced them; no one had ever sung them to me when I was sleepy, when I was scared, when it was dark; they weren't really meant for me, they didn't belong to me. They didn't stay lodged in the place where your heart beats and where memories form. As I tried to share them with my child, I felt as though I was pretending to sing lullabies, simulating gentleness and tenderness, faking closeness. I couldn't be this ventriloquist mother.

I didn't have a mother tongue anymore, just imitations of sad, monotonous chants. So when night came, my son went to sleep for years to the slow and meticulous recital of the alphabet, repeated as many times as necessary. Night after night, as I rocked him on an old wooden chair I'd snapped up at a garage sale, I softly sang him the only thing I'd really appropriated: the alphabet song. Letters, all the letters, that's all I found to give him to calm him down against my breast as the day waned. *A-b-c-d-e-f-g. H-i-j-k-l-m-n-o-p. Q-r-s-t-u-v-w. X-y-z. Je connais mon alphabet, c'est à toi de le chanter.**

---

* I know my alphabet, now you sing it (or: Now I know my ABCs, next time won't you sing with me.)

Love can move mountains[88]

ONE DAY, WITHOUT WARNING, WHEN I WAS ALREADY IN MY thirties and pregnant for the second time, my mother showed up at my house with a plastic bag in her hand. Inside were the contents of her dresser drawer, so many of our little treasures collected over the years. Everything was there. My swimming medal, the mental-calculation contest certificate, the newspaper article with my picture, the Valentine, the short story contest prize, the rhyming poems, and the acrostics. More than two decades of sorting, selecting, and streamlining, to end up with this plastic bag from Jean Coutu.[89] I wouldn't have to find this tribute to our childhood upon her death while emptying the house in a state of anguish. My mother handed over this bag of nostalgia as if she had resigned from her position.

She and my father had separated, she was moving for the third time in as many years, and she wanted to get rid of as much extra stuff as possible. At sixty-five years old, she was taking back control of her life, and this also meant shedding what she'd put up with for us, the weight of sacrifices borne during all those years far from her native country, from her home, so that she could give us more freedom. She was therefore returning this symbol of her sacrifice, an act that seemed to say, "My work is done, I'm going to try to find out who I am now that I don't have to come last anymore." The bag a last offering, the legacy of this period now safely behind her.

Once she left, I opened the bag and found myself thinking more about her than about myself. The rare memories I had of her in Chile came back to me, indelible. My mother singing in a loud voice as she played the guitar on our front step. Her black hair, loose and wavy. How she'd put on a costume to do a children's play with her sister, the actress. The way she burst out laughing, gossiping with her friends. Her keen appetite and obvious joy as she ate avocado on toast and pastries at tea time. That's the image I have of my mother in Chile, a round, radiant, loud, and exuberant woman who played the guitar badly and unabashedly, in front of the whole street, when the days were sunshine, and she was summer.

I found an unbelievable number of old drawings in the bag. Among them was the last one I'd made in the land of my birth. My mother had carried it all the way here with the few other things that fit in her suitcases, and had preciously hung on to it for all these years. It was from December 1986, barely a few days before we left Chile for good. It was for Santa Claus. There was a little girl with a large, confident smile; in the background, of course, there were mountains. I recognized them. All Chilean children draw mountains; the Andes cordillera is our horizon. It's where our gaze comes to die. Yet in my subsequent drawings, the mountains disappeared.

In my apartment on the Plateau, a baby girl in my womb and a bag of memories in my hand, I wondered about the precise moment I had stopped seeing mountains in my head. When had they stopped constituting the boundaries of my world? It occurred to me that they must have gradually disappeared behind the snow squalls of our Canadian winters. Buried under the weight of the cold when we crossed the border. When we arrived in Montreal. When I learned French. When my mother dyed her hair blond to look more Québécoise. When I stopped wanting to go to church with her. The snow must already have covered the Andes when, as a cleaning lady, she stopped hoping she'd ever work with children again someday.

Although she's still very beautiful and charming, with a mischievous glint in her eyes, the woman who handed me the Jean Coutu bag is much thinner than the one from Chile, and she hasn't played music for at least a quarter of a century. Not knowing when the cordillera deserted my childhood drawings scares the shit out of me, but I also know that in the drawings that followed, there was no longer anything blocking the horizon. I realize that my mother's love moved mountains, and not just any mountains. The whole cordillera.

EPILOGUE

Je me souviens[90]

IN MY MEMORIES, EVERYTHING WAS CLEAR. I WAS WATCHING the news with my father in the rear room of our apartment on Sainte-Catherine East, the room that looked out onto the street. I was half-listening, while leafing through a book, until the moment they announced Pierre Dufresne's death. The strapping fellow who played Fardoche had succumbed to a heart attack. The picture on Radio-Canada displayed his scarred face and his big body, which had once so impressed me. That imposing presence of his. I didn't really use to like him that much, he actually frightened me a little, so his death didn't exactly devastate me. But they were talking about my favourite show. Fardoche was dead. For once, I found what was happening on TV relevant to me.

The next evening, turning on the TV, I nevertheless saw Passe-Montagne, playing the spoons, accompanied by Fardoche the Farmer, his big hands hitting the tambourine to the rhythm of a song about growing vegetables.

I was stunned. I tried very hard, but I couldn't figure it out. The day before, there had been a big, emotional homage on TV. Today, before my eyes, I could see him laugh his big, ringing laugh.

I went to see my father. "Papa, do they tell lies on the news in Canada?"

"Why do you ask?"

"Is Fardoche dead?"

"Yes."

"But look! He's there!"

"Caroline, *es un actor*. He's an actor!"

"Yes, I know, but he's alive! He went to work at *Passe-Partout*!"

"What are you talking about? That was filmed before."

I clearly remember that the next day, at school, I was very excited to tell everyone of my revolutionary discovery. "Guys, what you see on TV isn't really real. IT'S FILMED BEFORE!" I was so keen to spread this news. Our lives are real, more real, more live than on TV: let's live them!

I was so amazed. I'd just realized the extent to which TV was an illusion. That what we watch is not real, not even the now. Not a window on the present, just a story they taped and played for us afterwards. I saw Fardoche come through the screen with his plaid shirt and his basket of vegetables, but he didn't exist anymore. He never would exist anymore, and yet he continued singing. As I recall, the song was about being a head of lettuce and wanting to be eaten. My revelation haunted me for weeks. Even today, I consider this a pivotal moment in my transition from childhood to adolescence.

After that episode, I was never able to watch TV the same way. From then on, I'd view it with a jaded eye. *Yeah, yeah, keep talking, I know your tricks, you aren't going to impress me, you're just replaying these stories for me when you feel like it.* I knew I'd been betrayed, but I was also enthralled: the small screen disconcerted me. Fiction was sourced from the flesh of real individuals, but it continued to speak and recite even once these people were dead and buried. How could that have more importance than real lives that went ignored?

As I was writing this book, Fardoche managed to surprise me again.

I did a bit of research on *Passe-Partout*, just to make sure I was getting certain details right. What I discovered left me stunned.

Pierre Dufresne died in 1984.

I was four years old at the time.

I was living in Chile.

I had not yet heard a single word of French, and Canada was not in my family's plans.

There is no way I saw his death being announced on the news, or that his appearance the next day had stupefied me. It's even less possible that I talked about it with my whole class two days later. It is absolutely impossible.

At first, I thought I was crazy, that I'd replaced my real memories with a bunch of nonsense. Then it occurred to me that I must have so thoroughly appropriated this culture that I'd mentally planted myself in Québec before even setting foot here. What had I erased from my mind so that Pierre Dufresne could cling to my memories instead? Did the seven-year-old girl who hadn't balked when told her life in Chile was over actually die a little, in the end, as she left the country? Was it like repotting a plant, I had to embrace a new life by forgetting my old one, starting again, tabula rasa? They often say that memories are not formed before the appearance of language. My language is now French; it intruded and prevailed, destroying everything that preceded it. So what I remember is from here. I don't know what to think of this image that is somehow still so vivid.

Is it a dream? Made up? False?

And yet, it's part of who I am.

This imagined anecdote remains at the foundation of my identity, my relationship to the world, my life's storyline. As I dust it off, I realize that memory sometimes chooses laborious roads. It finds its source where words appear. Memories are fertilized and sprout like perennials. Today I acknowledge that I am not only writing my story but rather that these stories have written me and have formed the roots from which I've grown.

ENDNOTES

1. *Residencia en la tierra* (Eng: *Residence on Earth*): A three-volume poetry collection by Chilean author Pablo Neruda written over two decades, from 1925 to 1945.

2. *"Dans un grand Bœing bleu de mer"* (Eng: "In a big, sea-blue Boeing"): Lyrics from the 1976 song *"Je reviendrai à Montréal"* (Eng: "I'll come back to Montreal") by Robert Charlebois (b. 1944), OC, OQ, a Québécois author, composer, musician, performer, and actor.

3. *"Les étoiles du nord nous rappellent la mort"* (Eng: "The northern stars remind us of death"): Lyrics from the 2002 song *"Balade à Toronto"* by Jean Leloup (1961), a Québécois singer-songwriter and author.

4. *Passe-Partout* (Eng: The term for a master key, literally means "go anywhere"): The name of a Québécois children's television show (and of its central character) that ran from 1977 to 1992 on Radio-Québec and Télévision Radio-Canada.

5. *Cité libre* (Eng: "Free city"): An influential political journal from Québec. Founded in Montreal, the publication ran from 1950 to 1972, and again from 1991 to 2000.

6. *La liberté n'est pas une marque de yogourt* (Eng: "Liberty isn't a brand of yogourt"): The title of a 1995 book of essays by Pierre Falardeau (1946–2009).

7. *"C'est l'histoire du petit castor"* (Eng: "This is the story of the little beaver"): Lyrics from the theme song to the Japanese animated series *Le petit castor*. Distributed by Radio-Canada, the series was dubbed into French and ran from the 1970s to the 1980s.

8. A four-and-a-half: An apartment with four rooms, typically two bedrooms, a kitchen, and living room. The half is the bathroom.

9. COFI: Acronym for the Centre d'orientation et de formation des immigrants (Eng: Centre for the orientation and training of immigrants).

10. *Maya l'abeille* (Eng: *Maya the Bee*): A German-Japanese animated series based on a German children's story by Waldemar Bonsels, published in 1912. Distributed by Radio-Canada, the series was dubbed into French and ran from the 1970s to the 1980s.

11. *Touftoufs et les Polluards* (Eng: *The Smoggies*): Created by Pierre Colin-Thibert and Gerald Potterton, the French and Canadian animated series aired on Radio-Canada from the 1980s to the 1990s.

12. *Sur la rue Tabaga* (Eng: *On Tabaga Street*): An educational Québécois children's show that ran from 1989 to 1995 on Canal Famille.

13. *La bande à Ovide* (Eng: *Ovid's Gang*): A Canadian-Belgian animated series distributed by Radio-Canada that ran from the 1980s to the 1990s.

14. *Bibifoc* (Eng: *Seabert*): A French animated series created by Jacques Morel, Éric Turlot, and Philippe Marin that aired in Quebec in the 1980s and 1990s on Super Écran and Canal Famille.

15. *Madame Pepperpote* (Eng: *Mrs. Pepperpot*): A Japanese animated series by Studio Pierret and Gakken, based on Norwegian author Alf Prøysen's stories for children. The series aired in Québec on Radio-Canada from the 1980s to the 1990s.

16. *Hachi* (Eng: *Hachi: A Dog's Tale*): 2009 children's film by Lasse Hallström.

17. *Les mystérieuses cites d'or* (Eng: *The Mysterious Cities of Gold*): An animated television series created in collaboration with France, Japan, and Luxembourg, adapted from the 1966 novel *The King's Fifth*, by Scott O'Dell. While set in the sixteenth century, the series includes elements of fantasy and science fiction alongside certain factual elements of the pre-Colombian Americas.

18. *"Un ours polaire dans l'autobus"* (Eng: "A polar bear on the bus"): Lyrics from the 2006 song "Montréal -40C," by Malajube.

19. Super Carnaval; Super C: A Québec discount supermarket chain founded in 1982.

20. Rossy: Located primarily in Québec, the Canadian chain of variety stores was founded in 1949.

21. MUTC STM: The Société de transport de Montréal operates public transportation services in Greater Montreal.

22. *"Au clair de la lune"*: An eighteenth-century French folksong.

23. *"Ma p'tite Julie"* (Eng: "My Little Julie"): Lyrics from the 1993 song "Julie" by the band Les Colocs (Eng: The Roommates), a Québécois rock band formed in 1990 and fronted by Dédé Fortin (1962–2000).

24. *Mangeux de marde* (Eng: Shit-eaters): A Québécois insult for disreputable people.

25. *"Travailler c'est trop dur"* (Eng: "Working's Too Hard"): Song by Zachary Richard (b. 1950), a Franco-American Cajun musician from Louisiana. He is an Officier de l'Ordre des Arts et Lettres de la République française and a member of the Ordre des Francophones d'Amérique.

26. CIBC: Canadian Imperial Bank of Commerce, a Canadian multinational banking corporation founded in 1867.

27. *Le Bonhomme Carnaval* (Eng: The Carnival Man): Quebec City's winter carnival mascot, an anthropomorphic snowman sporting a traditional red *tuque* and arrowhead sash.

28. *"Dors, Caroline"* (Eng: "Go to Sleep, Caroline"): A 1989 song by Johanne Blouin (b. 1955), a Québécoise singer and songwriter.

29. A seven-and-a-half: An apartment with seven rooms, likely four bedrooms, a kitchen, dining room, and living room. The bathroom is the half.

30. Pop's charity truck: An outreach service provided by the organization Dans la rue (Eng: In the streets). The organization was founded in Montreal in 1988 to support at-risk youth and youth experiencing homelessness. Its founder, a Catholic priest named Father Emmett Johns (1928–2018), was known as "Pops."

31. The Jacques-Cartier Bridge: Inaugurated in 1930, the five-lane, steel-truss cantilever bridge located in the city's east end crosses the Saint-Laurent river and links the island of Montreal to Longueuil.

32. *The Peanut Butter Solution* (French: *Opération beurre de pinottes*): A 1985 Canadian children's film directed by Michael Rubbo.

33. Cégep: The French acronym for Collège d'enseignement general et professionnel. Cégeps are part of a publicly funded college system exclusive to Québec that offers academic, technical, and vocational programs.

34. Sister Angèle: An Italian nun who shared her recipes on Radio-Canada between 1981 and 1985.

35. Brother André: André Bessette (1845–1937), canonized as Saint André of Montreal in 2010. The lay brother of the Congregation of Holy Cross was an important figure to Québécois Catholics and was credited with miraculous healings associated with his devotion to Saint Joseph.

36. "*Dis-moi le nom de ton cavalier*" (Eng: "Tell me the name of your Cavalier"): From a children's skipping-rope game.

37. *École polytechnique*: A reference to an anti-feminist mass shooting at the Université de Montréal's École polytechnique that took place December 6, 1989, when Marc Lépine killed fourteen women.

38. Vachon cakes: Individually wrapped cakes, similar to Twinkies.

39. *L'avalée des avalés* (Eng: *Swallowed*): 1966 novel by Québécois author Réjean Ducharme, published by Gallimard.

40. *Chambres en ville* (Eng: *Rooms in Town*): A Québécois television series that aired from 1989 to 1996 on TVA.

41. Gregory Charles (1968): A Québécois pianist, singer-songwriter, choral director, television and radio host, and actor. He was appointed an Officer of the Order of Canada.

42. *La grande noirceur* (Eng: The Great Darkness): A phrase used to describe the oppressive era under Québec Premier Maurice Duplessis from 1944 to 1959.

43. *La bête lumineuse* (Eng: *The Shimmering Beast*): A 1982 documentary about moose hunting near Maniwaki, Québec, directed by Pierre Perrault for the National Film Board of Canada. The film premiered in Cannes.

44. "The woman who planted trees": A reference to the 1953 short story *"L'homme qui plantait des arbres"* by French author Jean Giono (1895–1970).

45. Cité Rock Détente (Eng: City Rock Relaxation): A Montreal radio station that played soft rock and existed from 1990 to 2011; today it is known as CITE-FM or 107.3 Rouge.

46. Bruno Pelletier (b. 1962): A Québécois singer and actor.

47. Julie Masse (b. 1972): A Québécoise pop singer.

48. Marie-Denise Pelletier (b. 1960): A Québécoise singer-songwriter.

49. Roch Voisine (b. 1963): A francophone country, pop, and folk-rock singer-songwriter from New Brunswick.

50. Ginette Reno (b. 1946): A Québécoise singer and actress, Reno is an Officer of the Order of Canada, a Chevalière de l'Ordre national du Québec, and a Chevalière de l'Ordre des Arts et des Lettres de la République française.

51. Marjo (b. 1953): A Québécoise singer-songwriter.

52. Gerry Boulet (1946–90): A Québécois musician and singer-songwriter in the rock group Offenbach.

53. Marie Carmen (b. 1959): A Québécoise pop singer.

54. Éric Lapointe (b. 1969): A Québécois singer-songwriter.

55. Luc de Larochellière (b. 1966): A Québécois singer-songwriter.

56. From the song, "Tu m'aimes-tu" by Richard Desjardins. In French, the words are: *Y est midi moins quart et la femme de ménage est dans le corridor pour briser les mirages.*

57. Gilles Vigneault (b. 1928): A Québécois poet, author, and singer-songwriter. One of his most notable hits, "Gens du pays" (Eng: "People of the Country"), is often considered Québec's de facto national anthem. Vigneault is a Grand Officier de l'Ordre national du Québec, Chevalier de l'Ordre national de la Légion d'honneur, and an Officier des Arts et des Lettres du Québec.

58. Félix Leclerc (1914–88): A Québécois singer-songwriter, poet, author, radio and television host, scriptwriter, director, and actor. Leclerc was a Grand Officier de l'Ordre national du Québec and Chevalier de l'Ordre national de la Légion d'honneur. The prize for best Québec songs is named the Prix Félix in his honour.

59. Marcel Pagnol (1895–1974): A French novelist, playwriter, and filmmaker.

60. *Mafalda:* An Argentinian comic by Quino published from 1964 to 1973, popular throughout Latin America, Europe, and Québec.

61. Prix Goncourt: A French literary prize created in 1892.

62. L'Euguélionne: A feminist bookstore in Montreal.

63. *Les catastrophes de Rosalie* (Eng: *Rosalie's Catastrophies*): A 1987 Québécois YA novel by Ginette Anfousse published by Éditions La Courte Échelle.

64. *Ani-Croche* (Eng: *Crooked Ani*): Serialized YA novels by Bertrand Gauthier first published in 1985.

65. Arlette Cousture (b. 1948): A Québécoise author of historical novels, notably of *Les Filles de Caleb* (Eng: *Caleb's Daughters*), published in 1985.

66. *"Savez-vous planter du choux?"* (Eng: "Do you know how to plant cabbage?"): A French nursery rhyme and children's song.

67. Madame Brossard de Brossard: A suburbanite character played by Québécois actor and TV host Guy A. Lepage.

68. Le collège Jean-de-Brébeuf: A private francophone high school and college founded in 1928 by Jesuits.

69. The Champlain Bridge: Inaugurated in 1962, the bridge crossed the Saint-Laurent river, connecting Montreal to Brossard. The bridge was replaced in 2019 by the Samuel De Champlain Bridge.

70. Espace Go: Founded in 1979 by Pol Pelletier, the Montreal theatre produces innovative works by contemporary playwrights.

71. *Bonheur d'occasion* (Eng: *The Tin Flute*): A 1945 novel by Franco-Manitoban author Gabrielle Roy about Montreal's working-class neighbourhood of Saint-Henri.

72. *"Ce soir, l'amour est dans tes yeux"* (Eng: "Love Is in Your Eyes Tonight"): A 1985 song performed by Québécoise singer Martine St-Clair, originally written by Claude-Michel Schönberg.

73. "Eat your socks": From the French *"Manger ses bas."* A Québécois expression that means a feeling of panic before a situation over which you have no control.

74. Serge Fiori (b. 1952): A Québécois singer-songwriter and the lead vocalist and guitarist for the progressive rock group Harmonium.

75. Garou (b. 1972): A Québécois singer and actor.

76. Daniel Lavoie (b. 1949): A Franco-Manitoban singer-songwriter and pianist.

77. *La Fureur* (Eng: *Furor*): A television game show that aired on Radio-Canada from 1998 to 2007.

78. Michaëlle Jean (b. 1957): Originally from Port-au-Prince, Haiti, the stateswoman has worked as a diplomat, journalist, and television host. From 2005 to 2010, she served as the twenty-seventh Governor General of Canada.

79. Kim Thúy (b. 1968): Born in Saigon, Vietnam, the award-winning Québécoise author and television host's works have been translated into twenty-nine languages. She is a member of the Ordre des arts et des lettres du Québec.

80. Dany Laferrière (b. 1953): Born in Port-au-Prince, Haiti, the award-winning author, academic, and filmmaker lives between Montreal and Paris. He was elected to the Académie française in 2015.

81. *Sábado Gigante*: A Spanish-language television series broadcast by Spanish International Network in the United States.

82. *La poule aux œufs d'or* (Eng: The hen with the golden eggs): A Loto-Québec game show that first aired from 1958 to 1966 on Radio-Canada and since 1993 on TVA.

83. Vilain Pingouin (Eng: Naughty Penguin): A Québécois rock band from the 1980s and 1990s.

84. *Le temps des bouffons* (Eng: *The Time of the Buffoons*): A short film made in 1985 by Pierre Falardeau (1946–2009) comparing the English rule in Ghana with Canadian dominance in Québec by showing the 200th anniversary of the Montreal Beaver Club.

85. Pierre Falardeau (1946–2009): A Québécois author, filmmaker, director, and activist for Québec independence.

86. UQAM: Acronym for Université du Québec à Montréal, part of a system of ten provincially run public universities throughout Québec.

87. Henry Morgentaler, CM (1923–2013): A Polish-born Canadian doctor and abortion rights advocate who opened his first abortion clinic in Montreal in 1969.

88. "Love Can Move Mountains": 1992 song performed by Céline Dion, written by Diane Warren.

89. Jean Coutu: Headquartered in Québec, the Canadian drugstore chain is also present in New Brunswick and Ontario.

90. *Je me souviens* (Eng: I remember): Québec's official motto, it is seen on Québec licence plates and thought to have been first popularized by Étienne-Paschal Taché (1795–1865).

ACKNOWLEDGEMENTS

FROM THE AUTHOR

Paul Moëll and Bérénice Moëll: You are the best people I know and the best part of me. You, children of light, are the ones who are bringing me up.

Jacob Moëll: *Du såg mig på kvällen, du såg timmarna och al den där tiden, du fans där alltid för mig. Du bereder bägen för mig i alla mina projekt, alltmedan du förvandldar våra barn till en prins och en drottning.*

Nicholas Dawson: my accomplice, my first reader, you were also the first person to tell me, "You're a writer," and as always, I believed you.

Natalia San Martin, Alfredo Dawson, Jim Dawson: immigration hit you the hardest, and it is your sacrifices that have allowed joy, abandon, and words to thrive.

Maryse Andraos: thank you for your gentle eyes each time I couldn't see clearly.

Rachel Bédard, Anne Migner-Laurin, Camille Simard, and Margot Cittone: You've been so sweet and warm that the first time I set foot in your offices at Éditions du remue-ménage, I knew I was home. Thank you for guiding me with such sensitivity.

My friends, my sisters: Jennifer Bélanger, Gabrielle Tremblay, Katia Belkhodja, Estelle Grandbois-Bernard, Johanne Lachance, Isabelle Bujold, Tanya Déry-Obin, Geneviève Bouchard, Julie Marchiori, Ève-Catherine Champoux, Valérie Blanc, and the women from FLJM: Valérie Léger, Françoise Conea, Karine Villeneuve, Ariane Leduc, Karine Fortin, Noémie Philibert-Brunet. I would never have written without the support and kindness of my circles of feminine strength. You are an inspiration.

I would like to thank my translator, who fell in love with my book and asked me, out of the blue, if I would like her to translate it. We can read all her love in her translation. During this process that needed many back-and-forth emails, a real conversation started, and a real friendship was born. Thank you, Anita, for our ongoing correspondence and all the love that you put into every word that started out as mine, but that you've made your own.

I would also like to thank all the Book*hug family, who since the beginning, with great professionalism and sensitivity, have been so understanding of my condition.

FROM THE TRANSLATOR

Thank you, Caroline Dawson, for writing this brave and beautiful book, for your enthusiasm and support for this project, and for your friendship.

Thank you, Melissa Bull, for your incredibly thorough and thoughtful edits.

Thank you, Jay and Hazel Millar, for all the amazing work you do and for your equally amazing patience and flexibility. And thank you for your trust.

Frédéric Samson, thank you for being my sounding board, and for everything else. You are so many meanings of good.

ABOUT THE AUTHOR

Caroline Dawson was born in Chile in 1979 and immigrated to Québec with her family when she was seven. *As the Andes Disappeared*, originally published in French as *Là où je me terre* (2020), was a finalist for various prizes, including the Prix des libraires du Quebec and Radio-Canada's Combat national des livres, and won the Prix littéraire des Collégiens and the Prix AIEQ. She is also the author of the poetry collection *Ce qui est tu* (2023). Dawson teaches sociology and co-organizes the Montreal Youth Literature Festival. She lives in Montreal.

ABOUT THE TRANSLATOR

PHOTO: ALEXIS LAFLAMME

Anita Anand is an author, translator, and language teacher from Montreal. She is the author of *Swing in the House and Other Stories*, which won the 2015 Concordia University First Book Prize and was shortlisted for the 2016 Relit Award for Short Fiction and the Montreal Literary Diversity Prize. Her novel, *A Convergence of Solitudes*, was nominated for the 2022 Paragraphe Hugh MacLennan Prize for Fiction and the 2023 Forest of Reading Evergreen Award. Her previous translations include *Nirliit* by Juliana Léveillé-Trudel, which was nominated for the 2018 John Glassco Prize, and the novels *Lightness* and *Mukbang* by Fanie Demeule.

COLOPHON

Manufactured as the First English Edition of
As the Andes Disappeared
in the fall of 2023 by Book*hug Press

Edited for the press by Melissa Bull

Copy-edited by Stuart Ross
Proofread by Laurie Siblock
Type + design by Michel Vrana

Printed in Canada
bookhugpress.ca